Grabbing Fae's wrist, Rick spun her back toward him and claimed her gasp with his kiss.

And not just any kiss—he forked his fingers into the hair that had been driving him wild from the second he'd laid eyes on her and plundered those lips that had done the exact same. He left her in *no doubt* that he wanted that kiss. That he wanted to taste her, explore her, understand every part of her...

That was the kiss he gave her.

And it burned him to his very soul.

By the time he dragged his lips away to suck in much-needed oxygen, he was no longer sure who had needed it more, but he needed to do it again. And again. And again.

"You have no idea how long I've wanted to do that for," he rasped against her lips, his forehead pressed to hers.

Dear Reader,

I've always wanted to write a romance where the four-legged friends are instrumental in bringing the hero and heroine together. Whether it's my childhood love of *101 Dalmatians* or furry friends in general, I knew it had to be done.

Throw in a sprinkling of enemies to lovers, a dash of *Pride and Prejudice* (Mr Darcy, swoon!), a gorgeous beach setting, and *What Happens at the Beach*... was born.

I threw off every shackle with this tale—the inner critic, editor, reader... I stopped second-guessing what everyone else would want from it and wrote what I wanted. I wrote for the sheer fun of what was happening on the page...or should I say, "at the beach," and it was magical!

I hope you find that magic when you read it...along with the special breed of joy Great Danoodles can bring ;-)

Happy reading, and enjoy Bondi!

Rachael xx

WHAT HAPPENS AT THE BEACH...

RACHAEL STEWART

Harlequin

ROMANCE

Harlequin®
ROMANCE

ISBN-13: 978-1-335-21629-8

What Happens at the Beach...

Copyright © 2025 by Rachael Stewart

Recycling programs for this product may not exist in your area.

 Harlequin Enterprises ULC
22 Adelaide St. West, 41st Floor
Toronto, Ontario M5H 4E3, Canada
www.Harlequin.com

Printed in U.S.A.

Rachael Stewart adores conjuring up stories, from heartwarmingly romantic to wildly erotic. She's been writing since she could put pen to paper—as the stacks of scrawled-on pages in her loft will attest to. A Welsh lass at heart, she now lives in Yorkshire, with her very own hero and three awesome kids—and if she's not tapping out a story, she's wrapped up in one or enjoying the great outdoors. Reach her on Facebook, X (@rach_b52) or at rachaelstewartauthor.com.

Books by Rachael Stewart

Harlequin Romance

Billionaires for the Rose Sisters

Billionaire's Island Temptation
Consequence of Their Forbidden Night

Claiming the Ferrington Empire

Secrets Behind the Billionaire's Return
The Billionaire Behind the Headlines

How to Win a Monroe

Off-Limits Fling with the Heiress
My Unexpected Christmas Wedding

One Year to Wed

Reluctant Bride's Baby Bombshell

Unexpected Family for the Rebel Tycoon
Fake Fling with the Billionaire

Visit the Author Profile page at Harlequin.com.

For Michelle Douglas, Amy Andrews
and Clare Connelly,

Thank you for providing a 24/7 Aussie Q&A hotline :-)
Love ya, Ladies!
xxx

Praise for
Rachael Stewart

"This is a delightful, moving, contemporary romance....
I should warn you that this is the sort of book that
once you start you want to keep turning the pages
until you've read it. It is an enthralling story to escape
into and one that I thoroughly enjoyed reading. I
have no hesitation in highly recommending it."

—*Goodreads* on *Tempted by the Tycoon's Proposal*

CHAPTER ONE

Fae Thompson dropped her solitary bag on the footpath and stared up and up and up at the three-storey building before her.

No. Freaking. Way.

She'd known Sasha was rich. Her stepsister, her stepfather, her entire stepfamily were sickeningly, toe-curlingly, 'roll around in bed and get banknotes stuck where the sun don't shine' kind of rich, but this…

She plucked off her shades and immediately shoved them back on again. Gave a wince. Was it possible even the sun in Sydney outperformed the sun in Melbourne?

And now she was just being plain ridiculous. But while the ocean rolled with its ostentatious roar against the impressive rocks behind her, the looming structure ahead with its white walls and abundance of sea green glass had officially become offensive to her eyeballs. Never mind her sensitized ego, which had taken something of a reinvigorated poking since Sasha's Big White Wedding a week ago.

And yes, the day needed capitalizing.

Much like Sasha's Big White Bondi Beach House before her.

Bitter, much?

No, Fae wasn't. Not really.

Sasha deserved every bit of the happiness she had found in her BFF turned wife. Gabriella, aka Gigi. A stunning supermodel who had finally seen the light, or rather the love that had been right in front of her all along.

To know that her uberconfident stepsister had been in love with her best friend since forever and had been too scared to admit her feelings… To have sat back and watched Gigi repeatedly fall in and out of love with others and been there to pick up the pieces, time and time again… All the while, loving her unconditionally and whole-heartedly and unrequitedly.

Fae felt the goofy smile on her lips and swiftly batted it away.

Love. Who'd go there? Not Fae, that was for sure. All those tortured and wasted years pining for another… Now she shuddered, any remnants of the smile thankfully dislodged.

But her stepsister was in love. Gigi was in love. Her mother and her stepfather were *still* in love. After four years of marriage and six years together. And Fae had given *them* a year tops. What was the world coming to?

And now Fae was here. Her own life unrecognizable. Her home and livelihood back in Brunswick East reduced to rubble as rich-ass developers rolled in and tore down the bar she'd worked in with Mum since she was fifteen years old. Her home above it too!

Not that Mum cared; she'd moved on—six years ago to be exact. It was Fae who hadn't. Fae who, at twenty-four years of age, didn't know what to do with her life. What she wanted out of it. Where to live. What to be.

For the last couple of years, she'd filled her spare time protesting the redevelopment project. And when that had become futile, she'd put her efforts into ensuring those around her had been taken care of. Her regulars at the bar as well as her more vulnerable neighbours in need of a new home that they could still afford to rent. Because Brunny East was on the up and so were the rents, pushing out the old tenants and bringing in the new. Ones with bigger purses, flashier purses. People like the Sashas of the world who could afford it. No thought given to those who had lived there all their lives and their ancestors before them.

As for the bar…it hadn't just been a place to enjoy a drink; it had been a place of respite for her regulars. She'd been there for them. A smile when they needed it. An ear when they wanted to talk. Quiet company when they didn't.

With it gone, where would they go? Were they as adrift as she suddenly felt?

'Can I help you?'

She started, blinking this way and that on the empty footpath. 'Hello?'

'You've been stood there for all of five minutes,' the disembodied voice continued, Fae's hackles rising with every plummy beat. British. Pompous. Male. Joy of joys. She'd had her fill of those of late. 'I'm assuming you're lost and in need of assistance.'

She spied a camera protruding from the neighbouring property, its red light winking at her, and cocked a brow right at it. 'Or that I'm casing the joint?'

Because she knew exactly how she must look to someone of his breeding. She didn't need to *see* him to know his kind. The kind that were pushing her out of her own neighbourhood back home. The kind that lived in houses like this. Right alongside Sasha. He was Sasha's kind… though to be fair, his property was quite different.

No less ostentatious but less blinding. A mix of wood and stone, softened with swaying palm fronds that peeked from a terrace overhead… She liked those, she begrudgingly admitted.

His low rumble brought her appreciation up short. Was he *laughing* at her?

'That too,' he admitted.

Flicking her choppy bob back, she jutted her chin out. 'I'm fine as it happens.'

She dipped to grab her bag. It was time to move and make good on her promise to Sasha—and get out of *his* eyeline.

She was here to house-sit for six weeks while Sasha yachted it around the Caribbean on her honeymoon, *not* get into a showdown with the hoity-toity neighbours on day one.

'If you're sure,' came that low, self-assured English drawl.

'I'm always sure.'

Correction. She'd always been sure right up until the time Mum got hitched and then all her sureness flew out the window with her Mum's 'I do'. And how was that for weakness?

Hitching her life plan to her mother's and the four walls they lived in without even realizing it?

Kaboom!

'Suit yourself.'

'Too right I will,' she murmured under her breath, striding forth, head held high, even if her pride wasn't.

Because hell, she knew she'd played herself for a fool the last few years. But she was making amends. She was here to get her life back on track.

If only she could find the keys…and no, that wasn't some fancy way of referring to the keys for getting on the right track. Though it might as well have been. She really did mean the physical keys to the physical joint. Because she was getting hotter and redder and she swore he was still watching.

They had to be here somewhere... What was it with rich people and having to make everything so bloody perfect it couldn't—

Ah, there! A discreet doorbell, complete with camera and key safe, was tucked into the side wall of the double ground-floor garage.

Tugging her phone from her pocket, she dialled her stepsister as agreed.

'Fae-Fae!'

As with nails down a chalkboard, Fae's insides curled with her outsides—toes, fingers, even her tongue curled into the roof of her mouth. One day she'd get used to her stepsister's pet repetition of her name. One day. *Maybe.*

She forced a smile through gritted teeth. She wouldn't be surprised if Sasha was watching her through the camera right now. Watching her, assessing her, finding her lacking...

Not fair, Fae. Sasha has been nothing but adorable *to you!*

Perhaps the adorable bit was the problem.

Fae wasn't used to people treating her adorably and being genuine about it.

The bigger the purse, the greater the insincerity too.

And they didn't come much bigger than Sasha's.

'Hey Sash.'

'You made it then?'

'Yes, I've made it.'

Approximately fourteen hours and very little sleep later, not that she would admit to being grouchy because of it. She had after all refused to fly to Sydney, turning down her stepfather's offer of the private jet to take the overnight bus, so it was her own fault her body felt folded in two still.

But then, she'd never flown anywhere, and she didn't plan to start now. She preferred to keep her two feet firmly on the ground, thank you very much.

'You get that, Fae-Fae?'

'Get what?'

'I didn't think so.'

Her stepsister's voice tinkled with loved-up cheer. Its default setting for the past year or so. Ever since Gigi had said, 'I love you too'.

'I swear you're only ever half with us…'

Fae bit back the retort *Says you!* and went with 'You were saying?'

'The code…'

This time Fae focused and breathed a sigh of relief when the thing slid open to unveil a key and what looked like an alarm fob. She took them out and closed it up again.

'I had a grocery shop delivered this morning with the things you listed…' Had the tinkle taken on a ring of distaste now? Fae bit back a grin. 'And Freya, the local dog walker, is returning Precious this evening, in time for her evening walk. So she'll be able to take both you and Precious down to the local park, show you around. It's timeshared so you can only use it—'

Fae huffed out a laugh. 'A dog sitter for the dog sitter? Really, Sash, you trust me *that* much?'

Because this was the real reason Sasha had asked her to travel almost a thousand kilometres north. It wasn't to make sure her precious abode was okay; it was to make sure her precious Precious was.

No pressure, Fae.

'It's not a question of trust, but as you said yourself, you've never owned a dog before and Precious is—'

'Precious, I know.'

She managed to suppress an eye roll as she headed for the house—not over her stepsister's love for her dog, but her lack of faith. Because she absolutely respected Sasha's love for her hound. She did… She just didn't quite get the obsessive worry. She was a dog. How hard could it be? Really?

The house, on the other hand…

'Tell me, is there a special way to open the gate or is it— Ah, never mind, I've worked it out.'

She spied an access reader to the right of the gate that came off the garage wall, the shape of which matched the key fob in her hand. She swiped it against the panel and hey presto, the gate popped ajar.

'You do remember you sent me a *looong* email with the dos and the don'ts,' she said as she pushed on through the gate, making sure it closed behind her. 'Along with where I can take Precious and when, complete with map.'

'Yes, but—'

'A list of where to shop, where to eat, where to grab the best takeaway coffee.'

'Yes, but—'

'And you know you're supposed to be on your honeymoon forgetting about your life here for the time being...'

Though how anyone could forget about a place like this was beyond Fae's imagination. She walked up the steps that led to the first-floor terrace, her mouth hanging open as she drank it all in. From the architectural masterpiece that was Sasha's home to nature's paradise that stretched out before it. Nothing to hinder the incredible view of the ocean that had to be worth a fair sum alone...

'It's why you asked me to come, is it not?'

She was barely aware of asking the question as she reached the last step, her eyes bugging out over the white stone platform adorned with designer sun beds, tables, chairs, fancy topiary bushes...

Jeez, the 'garden' was bigger than her entire apartment back in Brunny!

'Yes, you're right.'

'So will you trust me to do as you asked?'

She could imagine her stepsister's smooth complexion wrinkling up with worry. Not wanting to poke the bear but poking it all the same as she hesitated. Their sisterly bond still too fresh to test with the truth.

'I do trust you, Fae,' she said carefully. 'It's not that I don't.'

So, she wasn't on Fae-Fae terms now…*interesting*.

'But Precious has been my everything for the last five years. If anything were to happen to her… Well, she's my child really. I should have brought her with me, but—'

'But nothing!' Fae scratched away the sudden prickle in her neck. 'Seriously, Sash, it's your honeymoon! Time for just the two of you. The *two* of *you*. Get it?'

Her mother certainly hadn't wanted to drag Fae along on *her* honeymoon travelling the world when she'd headed off four years ago. Not that Fae would have gone. Not in million years. But still…

'Besides, the last thing Precious is going to want to do is be cooped up on a yacht for over a month.'

Now she was just making stuff up because she had no clue what a fancy poodle would or wouldn't like to do, but it didn't *sound* like the sort of thing a dog would enjoy—did it?

'And you can't blame Gigi for wanting you to herself, not after the year you two have had to get to this point. You deserve it, Sash, you both do, so please, let me take care of Precious and your home, and you take care of your wife.'

'My…my wife…' She could hear the smile in her stepsister's voice once more, and this time she was glad of it. 'It still feels surreal, I have to pinch myself every morning— Ow! Gigi!'

'Did she just pinch some sense into you?'

There was a rustle down the line, a giggle, and was that a—*smooch*?

'Hey Fae, how are you?' came the other woman's distinctively Spanish lilt.

'Hey Gigi, I'm all good.' She smiled, realising she now had an ally. 'Or I would be if you can get Sash to chill the heck out. She might be in need of an intervention. Do you want to hang up and hide her phone somewhere?'

'Don't even think about it!'

'Too late, I am thinking, and I am all for freeing you from your technology, darling.'

'Gigi!'

'Fine, but if you still want to join me in that bath I just lovingly poured, you need to step away from the device.'

'Ladies!' Fae blurted, short of cutting the call herself. 'TMI!'

'Sorry, Fae,' Gigi cooed. 'I'm backing away… but you have five minutes, Sasha, darling. No more. No less. Bye, Fae.'

'See you, Gigi. And you'd best go too, Sash.' Thank heaven they weren't on a video call. Fae's cheeks were on fire. And it wasn't that she was a prude, but she didn't need to know what her stepsister and her new wife were about to get up to. She really didn't.

'I will. There's just one more thing…'

Fae hitched her bag higher on her shoulder and crossed the terrace on the hunt for the main door. At least this *was* obvious. The grand glass door screamed, *Main event this way…*

'Yes?'

'Some guy has just moved in next door and I don't know much about him but…'

'Which side?'

'Side?'

'To the left or the right if you're facing the house from the beach?'

She slotted the key into the lock and gave it a twist. It turned effortlessly—surprise, surprise. Nothing like the lock on her old flat, which took a special combination move and a hefty shove to budge. Oh, how she missed it though.

'The left.'

'You mean the Brit?'

'You've met him already?'

Fae paused, her ears pricking over Sasha's perturbed tone.

'*Met* isn't the word I would use—he saw me on the footpath and asked if I needed assistance.'

'Did he now? Well, I'd appreciate it if you gave him a wide berth. Or more specifically, that dog of his.'

'He has a dog?'

'A great big hound of a dog who pounced on my poor Precious like she was a piece of meat.'

Oh, dear. The horror in Sasha's voice was enough to make Fae grimace. As for avoiding a repeat of the encounter, that suited Fae just fine. She had no intention of going anywhere near the guy.

'We'll steer clear, don't you worry.'

'Thank you! I've put her schedule on the fridge, so it'll be easy for you to keep abreast of everything. Food. Timings. Walks. The works. But any problems, you call me, anytime, day or night.'

'No worries, Sash. You relax and— *Holy guacamole!*'

Fae froze just inside the entrance.

'What's wrong?'

Her bag fell to her feet with a thud. A cloud of dust lifting with it. *Her* dust. *Her* dirt. Never Sasha's. Because, my God, this place was pristine. Posh *and* pristine.

She wasn't sure why she was so stunned. She'd *seen* the outside so she should have *expected* the inside. And it *was* Sasha all over.

But expecting it and seeing it were two different things.

From the golden herringbone floor to the white walls, to the mix of glass, soft wood and duck-egg-blue accents, the place was a coastal dream. The glass to the front framed the terrace with its panoramic view of the ocean, the glass to the rear framed the pool—the *pool!* Way bigger than she'd imagined and surrounded by a garden with space to dine at one end and sunbathe at the other.

And above her, a central atrium style ceiling bathed the entire space in light.

'Fae? What's happened? Where are you?'

She rubbed her sweaty palm against her torn denim shorts, not daring to touch a thing for fear of spreading her muck further, or worse breaking something…which again was ridiculous. She was living here for six weeks. She could hardly keep her hands to herself.

'You didn't tell me your house belonged on *Grand Designs*, Sash.'

'Is that a compliment?'

'It's a "this place is something else" comment.'

And Fae had never felt more out of place.

Or she had, a long, long time ago…

'It's home.'

'Home. Right.'

Something Fae no longer knew much about.

'I hope you'll like it there.'

'Sure.'

'You will enjoy yourself, won't you? You can help yourself to anything. Use whichever of the spare bedrooms you're most comfortable in. But the one next to mine has the best view of the beach and since you'll probably find Precious sleeping in mine, it might help her settle to know that you're next door.'

'I'll bear that in mind.'

'And thanks, Fae-Fae, really truly. This means so much to me. And Gigi. And Precious. We love you.'

She gave a choked laugh. For a girl who'd grown up wishing for a family, for siblings, for a father to consider her worth knowing…now she found herself floundering in the face of it.

'No worries. Now go.' She pulled a face—*hardly warm and sisterly, Fae*—and with a meek smile Sasha couldn't even see, she added, 'Enjoy that bath.'

'I will, just…send me updates, okay.'

'So long as you promise not to obsess over them, and only because Precious is your baby.'

'Thanks, Fae.'

'And I'll guard her with my life—no big grey heffa will get within sniffing distance of her. Not on my watch!'

Her sister giggled, just as Fae had hoped, breaking the tension she had unwittingly put there with her inability to respond like any normal sister would. 'Speak soon.'

And then she hung up, clutching her phone to her chest that still felt too tight to breathe. She understood it. The tension. The awkwardness.

She didn't trust the affection. She couldn't count on it. Her father had taught her that from day dot. There were no guarantees when it came to love.

Don't demand it, don't expect it, don't *anything* it, and then you can't get hurt.

Period.

It wasn't in Rick Pennington's nature to be nosy.

In fact, it was in his nature to be the exact opposite.

If it wasn't his business to know, consider him well and truly out of it. He knew well enough what it was like to have people prying into the nitty-gritty of your life. Sharing it as gossip for a laugh or their own social advancement or a pretty penny with the press.

His childhood sweetheart—ex-fiancée, for his sins—had shared her own stories over the years, the odd tale cropping up even now a decade down the line.

Maybe he ought to take it as a compliment that Zara still thought him worthy of comment. Though any hope she harboured of a reconciliation had sailed the day she'd walked with the threat of bankruptcy hanging over him and his family.

A poor reputation she could handle, a lack of Louboutins not so much.

And he was done living his life under some kind of a microscope. Part of the reason he was glad he'd upped and left London to make a home for himself here, on the other side of the world, where the anonymity was as surprising as it was blissful.

He also had the beach on his doorstep. The sun, sea and surf all at his disposal. Features his property agent had leaned into when closing the deal months ago. But the truth was he hadn't needed the hard sell. He'd been ready to sign on the dotted line long before she'd even spoken. Ready to leave London behind. It's grey skies, boardrooms, even the rolling hills of the Pennington country estate too.

Though he'd stuck it out for Christmas. More to keep Mum happy, but now he was here, had been for two months, and he was all about finding a new way of living…of laughing.

Because, to use his assistant's words, 'Lord Pennington does not laugh. Not ever.'

It was a simple statement made to a simple passing remark, and to this day Rick couldn't shake it. Because his assistant, Geoffrey, was right. At the age of thirty-one, he'd lost the ability to find the joy in anything. The excitement. The thrill.

Idly he stroked at the stubble along his jaw.

He wasn't missing his daily shave, or the regular trip to the barbers as he put less effort into looking so clean-cut. But he *did* miss the fire pumping through his veins. He couldn't remember the last time he'd felt anything close to a spark. There was the exhilarating hit of a workout in the gym or a hard run. The rush of a successful takeover bid. The unbridled joy he found when his charity that specialized in rare disease research made a groundbreaking discovery that could change lives, save lives even.

But the joy in the everyday, the ordinary... things that should make your mouth twitch up more than once on a regular basis...

With every social function, every date, every family engagement since his assistant had made their candid observation, it had become more and more obvious they were right.

Though seconds ago, when a certain pink-haired pixie had the gumption to outright suggest she was casing the joint next door... *Oh, yes*, something had definitely come alive inside. A sure sign he wasn't completely dead after all.

And though it hadn't been an all-out gut-rumbling laugh, it had been something.

Which was probably the reason she had him feeling all sorts of curious about her now.

That and the fact she looked about as out of place as he was... Two months in and he still felt like a guest within his own home. Like he'd soon be packing up and flying back out.

A nudge to his knee accompanied a low whine and he looked away from the security footage to take in his Great Dane's doleful look. 'Don't worry, Ralph, I'm not bailing. Not yet anyway.'

Those sad brown eyes blinked up at him, looking far too wise for almost a year on this earth, and he lowered his hand to scratch behind his dog's ear. That earned him another whine. He checked the clock. 'It can't be that time already?'

Though in Ralph's world, it seemed like every hour of the day demanded a whine of some sort. Each indicating something else on his very full rota of eat, sleep, walk, repeat…and he was doing his best to ensure Rick kept to the same.

Just as Rick's sister had hoped when she'd suggested he get a dog. Her answer to Geoffrey's comment when Rick had raised it over whisky one evening. He'd looked at her like she was mad. But then she'd calmly explained, it was something else to think about that wasn't work. Something that depended on him for food and exercise and couldn't be ignored.

'Unlike a woman,' she'd teased.

Because, of course, a man accused of lacking a sense of humour had to be a workaholic, and was therefore in need of something that would force him to find a life outside of work.

And she was right about one thing: it couldn't

be a woman. He wasn't interested in a relationship. And flings served a purpose to a point. But
he'd cleared up enough of his late father's messes
to find them oddly disquieting, let alone satisfy-
ing or fun.

So a dog it was.

And his sister had been right to tell him to get
Ralph. The Great Dane had brought him balance
and many an unexpected benefit.

Had Ralph gifted him a new way of life
though...?

'What do you reckon, Ralph? Is this living?'

Ralph lifted his head off his knee, where it had
happily settled with his petting, and gave a 'Ruff!'

'I thought so. Come on then...' He got to his
feet and Ralph eagerly followed suit. 'A run and
then dinner.'

Though as he exited his gate, he found himself
pondering Ms Pixie once more. Who was she?
What was her connection to the sun-kissed blonde
who owned the place? They certainly didn't *look*
alike.

He'd only had the 'pleasure' of meeting his
neighbour once. And yes, the encounter really did
need quotation marks. Not that he could blame
the statuesque blonde who had taken one look at
Ralph eyeing up her poodle like one might their
next meal and swiftly cut their conversation short.
Informing him that she wouldn't be around for the
next few weeks, that her sister was house-sitting

and that she'd swing by on her return and, 'ta-ta', dialling up her passing jog into an all-out sprint.

He'd have to teach Ralph some table manners if he ever hoped to get acquainted with his new neighbours.

But then who was to say that people got to know their neighbours in this part of the world? What did he truly know of Australian living other than what he'd seen on the TV as a kid? What did people say about the Aussies—friendly, right? Always willing to throw another shrimp on the barbie…?

Though the blonde hadn't seemed the type. To barbecue or to welcome him in.

Then again, Ralph had seen to that.

As for Ms Pixie, who had disappeared inside the blonde's pad, she seemed more cool chip-on-her-shoulder than warm cheer…and was *she* the blonde's sister? Really? She looked nothing like her. Dressed nothing like her. As for *their* first impression…

'Maybe you can win her over better than my voice did, Ralph.'

CHAPTER TWO

'I CAN STICK around a bit. I don't have another job to go to this evening…'

The glossy brunette eyed Fae's clenched fist around the lead and Fae slackened her grip with a forced grin. 'I've got this. You can go, Mikaela.'

Because the last thing Fae wanted was to be babysat by a girl who looked all of fifteen. Though she had to be at least eighteen for Sasha to have entrusted Precious to her care for the last few days. And she didn't have a mucky scuff or a hair out of place…neither did Precious.

How was that even possible?

She frowned down at the dog whose slender snout was stuck so far north it reached as high as her waist.

Did this dog even poo?

'Well, if you're sure. Here's her treats and poo bags…'

And there was her answer. How lovely. She took them with a strained smile. Now that was *one* job she wasn't looking forward to. But snuggles on the sofa might be kind of nice. To have some company again…

'Let me at least walk you back to the house.'

Fae's gaze shot up, cheeks burning. Did Mikaela really think her *that* incapable?

The house was almost within sight, a mere kilometre back up the winding coastal path… she couldn't get lost and more importantly, she couldn't lose Precious. They were attached. Where Fae went, Precious went. Easy.

Though since Fae had been the one pulling a face at the poo bag dispenser—a fetching pink with its designer branding liberally on display—she couldn't blame Mikaela for continuing to fret.

'Perhaps you ought to attach that to the lead so you don't forget it, here like this…'

She manhandled the dispenser out of Fae's grasp and used the gold lobster clasp to hook it onto the matching pink lead that she'd hung around her neck earlier. Because apparently, *this* lead was for confined quarters, aka looking good in the city. The retractable lead that Precious was currently attached to was much better for the dog-friendly beaches, parks and open coastal paths—go figure.

'There. Better. You don't want to leave home without them, else you'll be fined.'

'Fined, right. Of course.'

Two leads. Poo bags. Treats.

What could possibly go wrong?

Precious chose that moment to raise a sardonic brow beneath her perfect white bouffant. A hairdo that would require daily brushing. All by yours truly.

'Dogs don't have brows, right?' Fae murmured, without breaking eye contact with the haughty pooch.

'Oh, they do!' Mikaela cooed, clasping her hands beneath her chin. 'Not like us humans, of course, but they reckon it's all because of our domestication of the species. It's just another wonder of evolution!'

'A wonder indeed,' Fae muttered, under no illusion that she was being assessed and found wanting, never mind communicated with.

And there she'd been worrying about the house and fitting into it...not the company pushing her out of it.

'Yeah.' Mikaela hunkered down in front of Precious, gaining the poodle's attention and a tail wag to boot. 'It's where dogs and wolves differ... *You* clever creatures have developed muscles in your inner eyebrows to communicate with us, haven't you, beautiful?'

Fae watched as she gave Precious a kiss to the tip of her nose—*not* something Fae was about to repeat in a hurry. Did she not *see* where those things went?

And then Mikaela was back on her feet, quizzical expression returning with her gaze. 'Are you *sure* I can't walk you back?'

'I have your number,' Fae was quick to assure her, *both* human brows raised to discourage further objection. *See, I can work them too, Precious.* 'I'll call if I—*we* need anything.'

'Day or night?'

'Absolutely.'

Over Fae's dead body was she going to ring. How hard could it be? Seriously.

She'd dealt with drunken strangers. Out-of-control hen parties. Over familiar men and women with hands travelling where they shouldn't. All in a night's work at the bar. She could cope with one high maintenance pooch almost half her size at the beach.

Though to be fair, Precious standing on her hind legs would come close to her height…with her impressive hair, probably outreach her too.

'Okay, then, I'll catch you later. Bye, Precious. Bye, Fae. Lovely to meet you!'

'And you.'

'And don't forget to stick to the off-leash hours at the park…the rest of the time.'

She gestured with her hand around her neck and Fae started—harsh!

She means 'collar and lead' not 'choke and hold', doofus!

'Got it.'

She saluted and with one last look of blatant

hesitation, Mikaela jogged off into the sunset, glossy ponytail swinging, and Precious strode forward, determined to follow.

'Oh, no, you don't.' Fae tugged her back, correctly deploying the control button on the retractable lead—*Well, look at you go, a natural in the making.* 'It's home time for us.'

She started off in the other direction, happy to have done something right, only to find herself being jerked back by the unmovable four-legged mountain that was Precious.

'Come on, this way.' She gave a gentle tug on the lead but Precious was going nowhere. How could a dog with such skinny legs and tiny feet be so strong? Or should that be headstrong? *Surely* she didn't need to deploy treats already?

Though if it meant an easy life...

She opened the bag and was about to extract a 'tasty' morsel when suddenly Precious took flight, sprinting and barking and sending the treats spilling onto the footpath. Dogs came racing for a scrap, seagulls too, but Precious was off, Fae with her as she struggled to shorten the retractable lead and gain any traction in her thongs.

'No! No, no, you don't!' she hollered, trying to haul the pooch back. *'Precious! Sit! Stop! Heel!'*

They were causing a scene. *She* was causing a scene. She scraped her hair out of her eyes. Tried to right her sunnies that almost hit the deck. Wished she'd worn her running gear because at least *then* she'd look like she was supposed to be running. Instead her thongs were slapping the footpath machine gun style and drawing every eye in the vicinity along with a fair amount of sniggers too. And no wonder. She'd be laughing too!

Who was supposed to be walking who?

And then the view up ahead changed. Mikaela and her swinging ponytail were obscured by a half-naked bronzed god running towards her. A giant four-legged hound running with him, ears flapping, tongue out…

What *was* that? A grey version of Scooby-Doo? It was speeding up too! The attached bronzed god with it.

She'd never seen a man like him. Not in real life. And now she was running and gawping and the scene had shifted into slow-mo. His hair undulated with his stride. Dark and almost to his shoulder, with highlights from the sun or the salon—who knew, who cared, because *man*, he was half-naked!

A grey T was hooked into the waistband of his black shorts where he'd also secured the lead for his dog. Daring, but practical since it freed him to run.

And those arms, *that* torso, all those exposed muscles unhindered and rippling as he came towards her. Body slick, either by sea or sweat.

Again, who knew—who cared! He was glorious. In all his laid-back, surfer-like glory.

And then his eyes met hers…at least she thought they had… He was wearing shades that hid his gaze, but she *sensed* his attention, the connection, the sizzle… Her heart joined the drum of her thongs and Precious gave a bark. *Hell.* Fae wanted to bark. *Woof* indeed.

Bronzed god frowned. Grey Scooby-Doo barked. The barks became a repeated yap back and forth and before Fae knew it, everything changed.

They were no longer running. Mikaela had been forgotten. Precious had applied the brakes and some kind of doggy tango was under way. Their leads became entwined and she was propelled forth by a hot furry body, into a hot bronzed body! Chest to chest! The leads wrapped around their legs and tightened as the dogs chased one another around and around in a frenzied yapping, sniffing, excited-to-get-acquainted fest—and, *really*, was there any way to get out of this with her dignity intact?

Sunglasses askew. Hair in eyes. One palm pressed to one very slick pec. The other fisted around the lead so tight that her knuckles flashed white. She opened her mouth and inhaled summer. Sun and coconuts. How could he even *smell* delicious?

And none of this was helping. She went to speak but nothing would come. Probably because her breasts were pushed so far into her ribs it was impossible to make a sound.

Your breasts? You're kidding, right? Nothing to do with your wildly beating heart trying to climb up out of your throat now that you're squished against Adonis himself.

'I'm so sorry!' she blurted.

He lifted his sunglasses to unveil eyes so blue she was bedazzled anew and, *oh, my days*, never in her life had she used such a girly phrase as *bedazzled*. What was happening to her?

Bondi Beach had a *lot* to answer for. As did Precious.

'You know they have a button to stop the lead from extending quite so much.'

That *voice*…

Like an ice bucket, she was doused. Chilled to the bone as recognition coursed through her.

'It's you!' she declared, a very different kind of heat rushing to fill her cheeks as she struggled against the restraints, desperate to get away.

Though if she wasn't careful, she was going to land on her arse because her legs were well and truly locked against his. As was his arm around her waist.

He gave a lopsided grin that reignited a mutinous spark deep within her. *He is* not *charming, Fae. He is* one of *them.*

Not only that, he was Sasha's neighbour, which meant that grey hound… *Oh, God.* She shoved her glasses up as she glanced down at Scooby-Doo, now with its nose right up Precious's—

Crap!

'Precious!'

'I prefer the name Rick, but—'

'Can you get your dog out of my dog's butt?'

He blinked, brows raising as he followed her pointed stare.

'If I may be so bold, he's saying hello and re-turning the greeting yours delivered not seconds before when—'

'I don't care if it's tit for tat, can you just do it!'

Before my sister somehow learns of this and declares me a failure on the spot!

His eyes were back on her. She didn't need to look to know it. Could feel his burning blues penetrating her wild mop and she wasn't *going* to look because she also knew her cheeks were flaming, her freckles ablaze and damn if her tiny button nose would be too!

'Very well. Ralph. Sit.'

The dog made a noise akin to a grumble but promptly plonked his butt to the concrete.

'Happy?'

No, she was *not* happy. Because she looked like a prize idiot. And they were still pressed together like a strung-up duo of meat for roasting. Not that she needed to see an oven with the heat she was giving off.

And it was all her fault for not taking control of Precious sooner.

So perhaps you ought to quit giving him the evils and show a little gratitude…

So much for Ralph's first impression going down better. Ms Pixie looked about ready to burn his four-legged pal to the ground. Or…maybe not as slowly she lifted her chin, her gaze with it.

Those hazel eyes *seemed* to ease…or was that the effect of the setting sun, softening her depths from their aggressive fire to molten gold?

Had he ever seen eyes quite like those before?

The kind you could truly lose yourself in…

And what dreamlike sequence are you getting lost in now?

He reared back—well, as much as one could rear back when still chained to another's tiny frame. And she *was* tiny.

Now that they were this close, and he wasn't viewing her through a lens, he could appreciate just how small. Her smile only just reached his pecs…if that thin-lipped, upturned quiver was indeed a *smile*?

His own mouth twitched to life with his gut. Though he daren't laugh. Her knee was too well positioned for him to chance any humour just yet.

'Thank you.'

As far as thank-yous went that had to be one of the most forced he'd ever heard. It reminded him of his sister, Kate, when she'd been fifteen and forced to thank Great-Aunt Lottie for the 'fetching' dress she'd been gifted for Christmas and made to wear for the family New Year dinner. Though his knitted sweater hadn't been much fun either.

'You're welcome.' Meanwhile *her* dog was having a good old rummage at ground level now that Ralph had planted his obedient behind. 'Would you like to tell yours to do the same?'

Her cheeks flushed a delightful shade of pink again as she dipped her head to give a hissed *'Precious, sit.'*

Her nose ring sparkled up at him, a delicate hoop with a stud flower. He liked it. A lot.

Almost as much as he was enjoying this hilarious little exchange as Precious refused to take a blind bit of notice. Ms Pixie did a little jig against him, gesturing at the dog like it would somehow listen if she tried to act out the command…while still attached to him.

'Precious! Down! No, not down, I mean up, the other way. No, not that way, this way…'

Oh, this kept getting better and better. If they stayed like this long enough it wouldn't just be him laughing; it would be every man and his dog stopping to cast an amused glance their way.

'Come. Here!' She upped her wriggling. 'Look! For *goodness*' sake! Could you just…?'

And now she was directing her ire at him.

'Could I?'

He cocked a brow and wide hazel eyes pleaded up at him. 'The leads?'

He looked down at their tightly bound bodies. His half-naked, hers not quite but very much trapped against his, and if he could have managed it, would have slapped himself upside the head. What was he doing? Or not, rather!

She may have got the hump from the off, but he should have seen her extracted from his nakedness immediately. He blamed her pluckiness. Her eyes. Her hair. That nose ring...*all* the distracting qualities. But really it was down to him.

And he, a supposed nobleman by birth, a man of gentle breeding... If his mother could see him now... Granny even! He moved before his blush could consume him.

'Let me see...' He took in the state of both leads, tried not to notice the way her lightweight vest and cropped shorts left little to the imagination. 'I suggest we move like so...'

He threw himself into the tangled puzzle that they made rather than his tangled thoughts, guiding her this way and that. Much to the amusement of their dogs, who tried to join in one too many times.

When finally they were free he locked her lead for her and handed it back.

'You want me to show you how to do that so it—'

'I know how to, thank you.' She snatched it

to her chest, the cool chip fully reinstated to his dismay.

And there was that blush again. Delightful, though she probably wouldn't agree. She cleared her throat, forked her hair, which left it in more disarray than before, and still he found himself smiling. *Oh, Geoffrey, if only you were here now.*

'Come on, Precious, time to go.' And she was off, so fast it took him a second to hurry after her.

'Wait, you can't—'

She halted, one offensive brow cocking. 'Can't?'

'You're just going to go, no names being exchanged, no pleasantries?'

'No *pleasantries*?' she spluttered over a laugh as Precious yanked forward, trying to edge closer to Ralph. 'Could you be any more British?'

'I'd rather think I was just being polite.'

'Precious!' She hauled the sniffing poodle to her side. *'Will* you just *stop* with the whole butt sniffing.'

'You know if you let them get it out of their system they will.'

'Right. Sure. And in the meantime…'

'In the meantime, we can at least exchange names?'

'Names? Why?'

That spark in his gut was back, his mouth curving up and if he wasn't careful, the laugh was going to out itself and she wouldn't understand that it was a long-awaited occurrence. And once out, it likely wouldn't stop.

And then he'd probably look a tad demented too.

Which would really build on the whole splendid first impression…

'Because it's what people do…?'

'When they expect to see one another again, yes.'

'And we don't?'

She mumbled something under her breath that sounded an awful lot like 'Not if I can help it.'

'What was that?'

Her eyes flared, the betraying colour in her cheeks deepening. 'Nothing.'

'I could have sworn you said—'

'It's Fae.'

He smiled. A name at last. 'Now was that really so hard?'

'You have no idea,' she mumbled, giving the impression he wasn't supposed to hear that either.

'Fae…' Could there be a more perfect name for her?

'Without the *y*,' she swiftly added, and there was the defensiveness again. The fierceness too. So much so it had Ralph's ears pricking. Even Precious stopped with her sniffing to cock her head in their direction with a whine.

'Duly noted. I'm Rick.'

He held out his hand, determined to rescue the

situation for the sake of his gentlemanly reputation. Not for his ego, though that was taking a severe bashing the longer this went on. The bashing becoming a full-on trample as his hand hovered in midair for a second too long and he wondered whether she was going to ignore it entirely.

But eventually, she surprised him by giving it a swift shake.

He grinned. 'It's a pleasure to meet you, Fae.'

She gave him something of a smile in return. 'I'd say it's a pleasure to meet you too, but I don't make a habit of lying.'

'Ouch.' He choked on a laugh. A laugh that morphed into an all-out rolling chuckle and as expected, she stared at him like he was mad. But man, it felt good. So good to let it out.

It also felt good to have someone be so frank, so brutally honest...

He'd never met anyone like her. Even back in the day when his family's name had been mud, people would sooner whisper behind his back than be outright rude to his face. Even Zara.

Call him a sucker for punishment, a fool, but he liked it—he liked her.

'Shall we walk?'

Her eyes bugged. *'Walk?'*

'You look like you're heading my way? Back to the house? I assume as you were there earlier, you're looking after the place while the owner is away...which is why I also thought names might be useful. You know, in case you need to borrow a cup of sugar or…' *And now you're just making this up as you go along! Afraid she'll race off if you let her get a word in?*

So sue me, he mentally countered.

She shook her head and started to walk, and he fell into step beside her. Not that he had much choice as Ralph and Precious took it as a sign to stride ahead together and his waist was very much connected to the former.

'Sugar not your thing? Let me guess, you're sweet enough already?'

She gave a disparaging laugh and inside he cringed.

'I can't believe I just said that.'

'That makes two of us.'

What was wrong with him? And why did he care so much whether she wanted to walk with him or not?

He lowered his shades back into position and studied her out of the corner of his eye.

And what weird attraction was this? To be drawn to someone who openly disliked you in return? And why was it so funny?

'Stop it.'

'Stop what?'

'Stop looking at me like that.'

'I'm just trying to suss you out. If you prefer, I could take my lead from Precious…'

Her mouth pursed to the side but he was pretty

sure she was holding back a laugh. A *genuine* laugh. 'If you value what's in your boxers, I wouldn't even joke about it.'

'Fair enough. I don't think I've ever had someone take such an instant dislike to me before. It's lucky I have such a thick skin.'

'Don't take it to heart. I'm like this around your kind all the time. Even with Sasha.'

'Sasha?'

'Your neighbour. She's my stepsister.'

'Ah, the blonde.'

Of all the things to say, that was *not* it as she snapped her gaze away and lowered her shades.

'The blonde! Of course that's all you see when you look at her.'

'Wait, no, of course, not. It was just a way to differentiate her from you and—'

Her brows were lifting higher and higher with his rambling explanation, her mouth forming a tight pink line.

'You're right, I'm sorry, I'm sure I could have come up with a better way to describe her.' Not that anything was coming to mind right this second because he was flustered. And he was never flustered. He didn't know how to *deal* with flustered.

And it wasn't like he'd been crushing on her sister. Not in the way he'd been... He cleared his throat.

'Look, what I'm trying to say is that you're very much chalk and cheese.'

'Because that sounds so much better?'

'Why do you see that as a negative?'

'Because if you hadn't noticed my stepsister is stunning in every way.'

'And you think that in turn means you are not?' Her dark brows hit the sky again.

'Well?' he pressed, daring her to answer him.

Instead, she turned away and for a moment he thought she was done with the conversation but then she surprised him with a shrug. 'She is classically beautiful. She walks down the street and heads turn. It's just the way it is. I don't envy that attention.'

'But you envy her something?'

She didn't respond.

He'd tell her she was equally beautiful, more so in his eyes if she thought she'd hear it, but something told him she wouldn't. In fact, something told him she'd take it in entirely the wrong way, so he kept his mouth shut and spoke on something he knew enough about to write a book.

'I'd much rather get to know the person beneath the glossy outer shell…'

'Yeah, right,' she scoffed, 'I bet you say that to all the girls.'

'I'm serious.'

She flicked him a look. 'Show me a camera roll of your ex-girlfriends and I might choose to believe you.'

He gave a laugh that sounded more like a strangled cat as he realized she wasn't joking. 'You're serious?'

'Too right I am.'

Well, that wasn't going to work. Too short. Too condemning.

Especially if he was to show her Zara. Then she'd think him the opposite—anti blondes because of her. The ex-fiancée. The one that got away. Which of course he wasn't. Not in the slightest.

Zara had taught him a valuable life lesson. To trust no one. Not even those you think you know.

Hell, he'd known her his entire life. She'd been as close as family to him. But then his father had been the same. Worse even. Corrupt. Unfaithful. A drunk and a liar.

'Okay, that look tells me all I need to know.'

'No, wait.' He hurried after her as she picked up her pace once more. 'You've got it wrong.'

'Really?' She didn't look at him as she said it.

'Why does it feel like we got off on the wrong foot?'

'Perhaps because we did.'

'What I don't understand is why.'

She fell silent though the air remained charged with his question. The dogs on the other hand were merrily walking together in front. Noses occasionally nudging, content in one another's world.

'Look, Rick,' she said eventually, flicking him

a look behind her shades—and what he would have given to see her eyes, to get a glimpse of her true thoughts…or not, as the words that came next felt awfully false: 'You seem like a really *nice* guy and all that. But I seriously doubt we have much in common and I'm here for a few weeks, looking after Sasha's place and this one… And I just want to do what I promised her without any trouble.'

She paused as they reached the gate to her home and she gave him what could only be described as a weak smile. Was she suggesting that he and Ralph were trouble?

'I take it that's a no to me inviting you round for a spot of shrimp on the barbie then?'

She pursed her lips and her shoulders trembled. Was that another trapped laugh?

'There are so many things I want to say to that invitation…'

'A yes would be great.'

'I can't. I'm sorry. But thank you. Come on Precious, bedtime.'

And with that she disappeared inside, a reluctant Precious trailing behind.

Ralph gave a whine and pulled on the lead to go after them.

'I know the feeling, Ralph.'

Odd, but true.

Though she was living here for a while. Did she honestly think she could avoid him for that entire time?

They *were* neighbours. And though Rick wasn't nosy, he was persistent. When he wanted something, he was known for getting it.

And what he wanted right now was to understand his new neighbour better. Her obvious aversion to him right up there with the rest…

First his neighbour and now Fae. Though his neighbour's disinterest had been of the 'polite but too busy to stop' kind. Fae's was something else.

Even now he could feel his lips quirking, his gut sparking to life. He shouldn't *like* it. Only he did.

And he wasn't about to question it because he was trying to be a new man. A man who put living in the moment first. And maybe, just occasionally, acted on something simply because it felt good.

'Come on, Ralph, tomorrow is another day. We can try and impress them then.'

Ralph grumbled and Rick chuckled. 'My sentiments exactly.'

CHAPTER THREE

FAE SNUGGLED DOWN deeper into the billowy softness all around—money certainly bought a different level of comfort. And she ignored the judgemental niggle as she basked in it a little while longer. Unwilling to wake up.

Her dream was too much fun. *He* was too fun. The Brit with the cheeky grin. Eyes that sparkled with mischief as he leaned that little bit closer. His mouth so near she could almost taste it. His nose nudged against hers. Damp. Insistent. He growled.

He—*growled*!

She shot up, eyes wide, and Precious reared up with a whine.

'Jesus, Precious!'

She clutched her chest as the dog snorted and came back down to earth, her front paws narrowly missing Fae's thigh and bringing her nose to nose. Beady eye to beady eye.

'It's too early for that look, Precious.' Fae turned to take in the view of the ocean and the sun already high in the sky, the number of people already out enjoying the day. 'Or maybe not.'

It had to be close to midday. Had she really been asleep that long? No wonder Precious looked about ready to eat her alive. She had to be starving... *and* desperate to get out.

Day two and Fae had failed. Again.

She threw off the sheets, Precious inadvertently with them, and winced. 'Sorry, darl.' She gave the poodle a clumsy pat as she got to her feet. 'Let's get you out. Then I can mentally berate myself.'

Raking a hand through her crazy mop, she jogged from the room and down the stairs. Throwing open the sliding doors to the enclosed lawn to the rear, she let Precious out while she went about preparing her breakfast as per the schedule that had been stuck to the fridge door. She took a second to ponder the effort it had taken to draw it up. It was like the email only bigger and brighter and broken down by day.

Mealtimes—what she ate and when. Walk schedule—where and when. Toilet habits, brushing schedule... And right there in big bold letters across the bottom: 'AVOID THE GIANT GREY DOG NEXT DOOR!'

Fae grimaced. She'd be insulted if she hadn't already failed multiple times over.

The pad of feet behind her announced the return of Precious, and she plucked the bowl of meat and veg off the side and placed it in the fancy gold stand beside her. Took up the water bowl next to it and filled it while Precious tucked in.

'At least you're not complaining,' she murmured, placing the water down too and turning her attention to coffee.

She wasn't a huge breakfast fan, but coffee, yes. *Always* coffee. And since her head threatened to return to the dream she had been indulging in, she threw her focus into her sister's barista machine. Because she was a pro at making coffee, not so much making light with dreams she really shouldn't be entertaining.

Coffee downed, Precious fed and watered, they set off for their morning walk, albeit almost lunch walk now. They had gone three strides when Precious promptly halted, sitting herself down on the concrete.

'What's up?' Fae frowned at her. 'I know we can't go to the park until this evening now, but surely a walk along the path is better than no walk at all...' Then she looked to the sky. 'And what am I even doing talking to a dog?'

'Worried she'll talk back?'

She jumped and turned in one movement.

'Rick!'

He grinned that same grin from her dream. 'Having fun?'

'Fun?'

She looked from him to Precious, who hadn't budged an inch. Though the dog did lean in to give him a sniff and he gave her an affectionate stroke, adjusting the paper bag he carried into his other arm and away from the nose that reached ever closer… Sausages, perhaps? Bacon?

And no, Fae did not observe that big strong hand issuing the caress and wish it upon her own skin. Not for a moment. Though the Fae from her dream…

'Does it really look like I'm having fun?' she blurted.

'It looks like you're trying to move a mountain.'

Twice in two days…was this going to be her life every day for the next six weeks? Trying to move the unmoveable?

'We're late getting out.'

'I'd say she's going to cook going out at this time.'

'It's hardly that hot.'

'She's a dog with fur. And you've got to think about her paws on the hot pavement.'

Fae looked down and frowned. Surely it was her butt that was taking most of the heat right now. But her paws…*oh no!* 'I should have thought.'

'They don't sweat either, except through their paws, which is hardly ideal so perhaps she's trying to tell you something.'

She palmed her forehead and closed her eyes, took a swift breath. Precious would just have to go without her morning walk.

You had one job, Fae! One job!

And she couldn't even get that right.

'Hey, it's okay, you know, she'll survive.'

Her eyes snapped to his, expecting to find him laughing at her but he wasn't. His eyes were full of compassion, warm and dizzying with it. Looking ever more blue against his tan and the blue of his T, too.

He really didn't look like an arse.

He just sounded like one.

And that wasn't fair.

She knew it. Even as she thought it.

She knew nothing about him. And instead of giving him a chance, she'd lumped him in with all the rest…all the wealthy men and women over the years who had made her life a misery, her father first and foremost.

'But if it really bothers you that much, I have an idea…'

'You do?'

'Do you fancy getting wet?'

She frowned. 'Do I…?'

'Well, not you so much as…' He looked to Precious, who had got to her feet, her nose edging ever closer to the paper bag in his arms, which he lifted again as Fae shortened the retractable lead. She wasn't falling foul of that again. Whatever he had in there, Precious wanted and likely shouldn't get. Her morning walk, on the other hand…

'If it means this one gets her exercise, I'm all for it.'

'Great. It's a ten-minute drive. Just let me swap this bag for Ralph and grab the keys.'

'Wait, what?'

'Rose Bay is a few miles away. It's a twenty-four-hour dog-friendly beach. Perfect for this time of day. They can roam off the lead and use the water to keep cool.'

'You're going to come too?'

'Unless you want me to give you directions and you can see yourself there?'

'I don't have a car.'

'Then it's settled, I'll take you. It's really no bother. We were at a loose end today anyway.'

'I...'

You what? You really want to say no and sound ever more ungrateful?

'That's very kind. Thank you.'

But what about her promise to Sasha?

And which one, exactly?

Making sure Precious got her exercise. Or making sure that Precious didn't get set upon by 'the giant grey dog next door'?

Rock and *hard place* sprang to mind.

'Do you want to go pack her a water bottle and anything you need too, meet you back here in ten?'

'Sure.' She gave a tight smile. Because *of course* she knew what she was doing. *Not.*

He clearly did though. And she needed some of that dog owner wit right now.

Only some?

She looked down to find Precious cocking that brow beneath the white bouffant that didn't look quite so perfect today— *Oh, God*, she hadn't brushed her yet either.

And what was the pooch—telepathic?

'Okay, Precious, I could do with plenty. Now let's go get packed before your dainty paws fry, or that stubborn butt of yours...'

Rick reversed his van out of the garage to find Fae waiting on the roadside. Precious sat at her heels. Amazing how a dog could appear haughty without doing much at all.

He pulled to a stop, hopped out and slid open the rear door.

Ralph came forward immediately.

'You stay there.' He encouraged him back. 'You've got a friend joining you.'

Or not, it would seem, since neither Precious nor Fae had moved from their spot.

He frowned. 'What is it?'

She lifted her shades into her hair as she looked from the classic camper to him and back again, honeyed gaze sparkling in the midday sun. '*This* is your van?'

'Is there a problem?'

'*These* are your wheels?'

'How many other ways do you want to ask the same question?'

Her mouth quirked to one side—an *almost* smile. 'I *never* would have had you pegged as a man for the van life.'

He eyed his most recent acquisition with folded arms. It's grey-and-white paint job might be muted but it screamed fun all the way. 'What are you trying to say?'

'I... You... Well...'

He cocked a brow as he looked back at her. 'Well what?'

She coloured and dropped her shades. 'Okay, got it wrong. You *look* the kind. You just don't *sound* the kind.'

She had a point, sort of, because up until three months ago he wouldn't have been.

'Do you want to know the truth?'

'Always.'

'I haven't tried Wanda out in earnest yet, but I—'

'*Wait*. You called her Wanda?'

He angled his head, not sure whether to be coy about it or own his momentary return to Marvel fandom days. 'I did. You have to name your van. It's a thing.'

'*I* know it's a thing. I just wasn't so sure *you* would.'

'Because of how I sound?'

'And you went for a classic too?' she said, smoothly avoiding his question.

'If you're going to try it, you've got to do it properly.'

'Define your view of *properly* because I would have thought for someone like you that would mean a fully working toilet, shower, kitchen, air con…'

He started to chuckle. 'Okay. It definitely has the air con, a sink, something of a shower and even a portable loo, which I would show you but that feels like it oversteps first-date territory.'

She stiffened and he moved on swiftly. 'I did consider something a little more, shall we say refined, but when I saw this on the forecourt, I figured why spend more than I needed. And Ralph liked it. Didn't you, Ralph?'

Ralph gave an obedient woof, to which Precious responded in kind. 'Seems Precious likes it too.'

'What about you?'

She grinned, giving him all the approval he needed. 'You're full of surprises, Rick.'

'Good surprises?'

'What do you think?'

And with that she stepped forward, coming to an abrupt halt when her phone started to ring and she pulled it from the pocket of her denim shorts—a size too big, he'd say, from the way they hung so low. But who was he to judge, and besides, on her they worked, in a laid-back 'I don't care' kind of a way. The kind of way he was trying to get to grips with himself. Her grey vest top was the same. Hanging loose, showing off her midriff and the straps of a pale pink bra or was that a bikini?

She grimaced at the screen and cut the call, pulling him up sharp.

'What is it?' Or perhaps the more pertinent question should have been who?

'Nothing.'

'Do you want to call them back? We can wait...'

'No, it's fine.'

'Sure?'

'Absolutely.'

Ralph poked his head out of the van, and she bit her lip. Hesitated. 'Do you think Precious can come up front with me?'

He looked at Ralph. The front was usually his boy's designated spot, but since they were taking passengers he'd figured dogs in the back, humans in the front. But to stick Ralph in the back on his own hardly seemed fair.

'I'm not sure whether Precious is a nervous passenger so I'd best ride with her,' she explained, wrapping the lead around her hands and giving off *all* the nervous vibes herself. 'Perhaps if we swap with Ralph and I'll sit in the back with her.'

That sounded better, but...was it more about putting distance between them now?

'If you're sure?'

'Positive.'

They swapped places, Fae getting into the back with Precious while he settled Ralph into the front. The task took a lot more effort than it should have since his boy was far too interested in following the female contingent into the rear.

'Yeah, yeah, I know, mate, I'm with you. But you'll have plenty of time to get reacquainted at the beach,' he assured him, clipping his harness to the seat belt before settling himself into the driver's seat. 'You ladies all set?' he added loud enough for them to hear.

He checked them out in the rearview mirror and bit back a laugh. Perhaps the whole nervous-passenger thing hadn't been a lie either because if Precious sat any closer to Fae, she'd be on her.

'We're good,' Fae mumbled into a mound of white fur, pressing Precious away to offer a smile of sorts. 'You can drive.'

'Excellent.'

He pulled out onto the road and set his playlist going—a chill-out mix from the noughties. 'This okay for you?'

'Mm-hmm.'

He checked her face, what he could see of it with Precious still doing her best to suffocate her. She appeared to be watching the world go by. Though he sensed she was deep in thought. For someone who was probably midtwenties tops, the crease between her brows seemed etched in.

Like she carried the weight of the world on her shoulders day in, day out…

'So, where do you live when you're not house-sitting for your sister?'

'*Step*sister.'

'Sorry.' So that was a touchy subject—there was a story there, if he ever got to know her well enough to learn it. 'Stepsister.'

'It was always just me and Mum growing up,' she offered by way of explanation. 'No family but us.'

'And where was that?'

'Melbourne. That's where I've just come from, Brunswick East.'

'I've never been. I've been to Melbourne a couple of times, but not Brunswick East. What's it like?'

'I loved it.'

'Loved?'

She met his gaze in the rearview mirror and immediately looked away again. Did she fear giving too much away? Coming across as vulnerable not her bag? What was it with the whole tough exterior? Did it make her all soft on the inside? He'd like to think so…

And why, exactly?

He'd clearly been in his own company far too long…

'You don't have to tell us if you don't want to, but we make good listeners, don't we, Ralph.'

Ralph gave a whine and he reached out to stroke his head.

'It's not been the same since the rich-ass developers rolled in and tore down the strip…'

He recognized that edge to her voice. The bitterness. It wasn't too dissimilar to how she'd spoken to him. Did she see him as one of them? A 'rich-ass' developer? All because of how he sounded?

'I'm sorry to hear that.'

'Are you?' she bit out before pressing her lips together, her eyes once more flicking to his in the mirror. 'Sorry, it's…it's a little raw, that's all. They've taken my job, my home…' She shrugged and Precious harrumphed at being displaced. 'Sorry, darl.'

She hooked her arm beneath the poodle's neck and gave her a scratch. 'I'm trying to find my feet again but it's hard when everything you've known is no longer the same.'

He gave a grim smile. 'I hear you.'

'Do you?'

He could hear the doubt in her voice. She didn't think he could possibly understand and yet he did because he'd been there. He'd almost lost both his home and his family as he knew it, his job too. A decade ago now, but the fight to keep it would stay with him until the day he died. It was likely the reason he'd lost the thrill in the very thing he'd fought to get back—his life.

He loosened his grip around the unforgiving wood of the classic steering wheel. 'Been there and bought the T-shirt. If you want to talk about it, consider me well versed and willing to listen.'

'Really?' The crease between her brows deepened with her surprise. 'Is that why you're here? Making a new life on the other side of the world? You lost your job and your home back in England?'

'I almost did once.'

Now she was interested.

'I managed to save the family home and the family business, eventually. But for a long time I wasn't sure I'd be able to. I lived with that risk hanging over me and my family for many years.'

'You were lucky you had the opportunity to save them.'

'Lucky?' *Lucky* wasn't the word he would use. Not when he'd been labelled an outcast. His father's behaviour had cast a shadow over everything he did. Banks turned him away left, right and centre. Investors wouldn't trust him. Supposed friends wouldn't. No, he hadn't been lucky. Not by a long shot.

'Well, you kept them, didn't you? Me, on the other hand... I fought to keep the bar. I fought to keep the flat. I fought to keep a safe space for the customers who've been coming to me for almost a decade but would anyone listen? Not the banks. Not the council. No one. Because I am a no one. And the people I'm worried about, they're nobodies. They don't have the money that talks. I don't have the money that makes people listen. So we just slip under the radar.'

And now he understood. The chip on the shoulder. The attitude he'd been getting from day one. The reason she wanted nothing to do with him… perhaps even the envy she'd been throwing at her sister too. Because it hadn't been about her stepsister's classic good looks or where she lived; it had been about her wealth. The wealth that made people stand up and take note.

'I see.'

'And now you sound just like them again.'

'Huh?'

'The bank. The council. Those with the money *and* the influence. I tried to plead with them all. And they all said, "I see." And "I'm sorry." Right before telling me they couldn't help. That it was best for the area and therefore best for the people in the long term for the redevelopment to continue. Even my stepfather when I went to him as a last resort. He had the contacts, the lawyers, he could have made a difference, but he chose not to. They even convinced Mickey in the end.'

'Mickey?'

'My boss, the guy who owned the bar. Though neither of us had a choice in the end. The bar, my flat, we were in the minority, the building was going.'

'Is it possible that they're right?' he dared to say.

'Why don't you ask the people who have lived in the area all their lives and now can't afford the rent on the pokiest of flats? And those who are lucky enough to keep a roof over their head, who will struggle to afford the kind of prices these developers seem to think they can charge in their hoity-toity wine bars and food joints? And don't get me started on the older generation whose kids and grandkids are being pushed out into the surrounding suburbs, because they can't afford to live close by. Leaving them alone in their later years. The number of customers I had swing by our bar towards the end bemoaning the situation… We all knew what was coming. I just never expected it to be so…final.' She gave a choked laugh. 'Stupid really, considering they were one and the same.'

'They?'

'My flat and the bar being in the same building. One bulldozer. Job done. Once the developer had it in its sights, it was only a question of time.'

'How long did you have?'

'Not long enough.'

'They must have given you due notice…'

'Oh, yes, they served notice, all right, followed the letter of the law, dotted the i's and crossed the t's, but no amount of notice can prepare you for having to upend your life. Mickey was sorry, of course, but he had Bali and his sweet retirement in his sights, and I couldn't hold that against him.'

With each word her voice had thickened, catching on the last. So much emotion. All for the job she had lost, the home…

She was looking out the window, either to avoid Precious's fur or to avoid his eye, but he swore he could see tears.

'And what about your mum, where's she living?'

Her lashes flickered and her throat bobbed and there was the pain, the true pain. 'Wherever her dreams take her.'

Oh, God…

Her eyes shot to his in the mirror. Had he gasped?

'She's not *dying*!'

'Sorry, it's just…' He pulled the van to a stop at a red light and gave her reflection his full attention. 'When you said it like that, all weepy and wistful, I thought…'

'Yeah, well, no, that's not what I meant…' She swiped at her cheek—a stray tear, he'd bet. 'I meant she's off travelling the globe with Tim—my stepfather—who's made it his mission to ensure she follows her dreams and sees every location on her bucket list…a thousand times over if she so desires.'

Beneath the derogatory thrum and the roll of

the eye, he could sense the appreciation, relief even… She was happy for her mum. Stepfather's obscene wealth aside, she was happy.

'Sounds fun.'

'Considering it was her lifelong dream to travel but she never thought she'd step foot out of Melbourne, it's more than just fun. And I'm happy that she's happy—that's all that matters. I'm *not* weepy.'

He opened his mouth to argue back but the words wouldn't come. Silenced by the emotion still shining in her eyes. The raw passion in her depths.

'I just…' She pressed her lips together, her nostrils flaring with her breath. 'I miss her.'

Her open confession reverberated through him and he turned in his seat, needing to look at her without the distance of the mirror. Even Ralph turned his head with a gruff rumble.

Her hazel eyes glistened and she gave the smallest of smiles, the smallest of shrugs. 'Pathetic, right. A grown-ass woman and I miss my mum.'

'That's not pathetic, Fae.' He gritted his teeth, swallowed against the ache building in his chest. 'Far from it.'

The aura she had about her. The restless sense of being at sea. That permanent crease between her brows. It made so much sense now. He wished himself beside her, wished his arms around her so that he could somehow absorb some of it.

Offer her warmth and comfort and companionship, even for a moment. Because he'd been there. Those days after he'd lost Zara, his friends, his father…

A horn sounded and his head shot up with a curse. He was supposed to be driving. Not acting as counsellor, getting lost in his passenger and his own past.

He twisted back around and checked the lights. Green. No surprise there.

Waving an apologetic hand out the window, he rejoined the traffic ahead. Waited for the mood within to calm before saying, 'So, your mum's off travelling the globe with her man, happy with her new lot in life. What about you? What's next for you?'

Nothing.

Had she even heard him?

He glanced at the mirror to find her idly stroking Precious, who had dropped into her lap, likely sensing the same as him. That need for companionship, for comfort…

He was convinced Ralph would've joined them too given a chance.

'Who knows,' she said after a long pause. 'I don't. It's why I'm here. Helping Sasha while I work out it out. Where I want to live. What I want to do. Who I want to be.'

'Sounds exciting,' he tried to inject enthusiasm

into his voice, into the air that still felt laden with it all. Her past and his. An unknown future too.

'You think?' She choked on a laugh. 'Not terrifying?'

'Maybe you just need to look at it in a different light, see it as an opportunity for a fresh start.'

'A fresh start...'

And then she smiled at him in the rearview mirror, and it was like the sun coming out from behind the clouds, warming him through and almost making him miss the turning to the car park.

'Okay then, Mr Insightful, if you're so hot on hope for the future,' she said as he pulled into a space, 'why don't you tell me what you're doing here so far from home? You don't sound like you've been in Aus all that long, or does an accent like that just stick around like a bad smell?'

He yanked the handbrake up, wishing to park the conversation more than the van. But he'd asked for it—poking into her life, her family, her past—so he owed her a bit of his own. And as he glanced over his shoulder and saw the teasing sparkle chasing away the shadows in her eyes, he found he no longer cared. It was a price worth paying.

'How about we get this pair in the sea first, and then I'll tell you whatever you want to know.'

Up came one dark brow. '*Whatever* I want to know.'

'Why do I feel like I'm going to regret saying that?'

'Because if I were you, I would be.'
She was serious and yet he was chuckling.
What the hell was wrong with him?

CHAPTER FOUR

THIRTY MINUTES LATER, shoes in hand, they were strolling through the shallows while the dogs lived their best lives jumping through the waves. So many other dogs getting involved too that it had taken a good fifteen minutes for Fae to trust Precious off the lead and the other fifteen to relax enough to remember the drilling she'd wanted to give Rick.

She cast him a discreet look as he raked his windswept hair out of his face, his eyes hidden behind aviators that reflected the sun back at her.

'You ready for the third degree?'

His mouth twitched up. 'And there I was thinking you'd forgotten.'

'Nah. I'm like a dog with a bone, me.'

He chuckled. 'So, what do you want to know?'

'It might be quicker to ask, what *don't* I want to know?'

'How about, "Where shall I start" then?'

'Easy. What brought you to Australia?'

It did *seem* like an easy question—something

he should have a ready answer for—though she'd sensed in the van that it wasn't. Not for him. And again now, as she freed him from her inquisitive gaze to take in the prancing dogs ahead, she could sense the tension in his six-foot-plus frame.

'It's quite a move from the UK,' she said into his silence.

'It is…'

Ralph raced up to them and dropped his soggy ball at their feet. He gave an excited bark and backed up as Rick dipped to pick it up without breaking stride and threw it, releasing some of the tension with it.

'At the risk of sounding like a cliché, I fancied a bit of sun, sea and surf. And since I can work anywhere in the world so long as I have decent Wi-Fi, Australia fit the bill.'

So he did work; he wasn't here living off his parents' money or rather bumming off his parents' money. She knew well enough that places like Bondi Beach were teeming with such 'kids' who refused to grow up. She was glad he wasn't one of them.

'Sun, sea and surf. You can't get that in the UK?'

'Have you ever *been* to the UK?'

She laughed. 'I've never even been on an airplane.'

'What, like never?'

'All right, all right, keep your pants on. It's not

that shocking. Plenty of people live their whole
lives without flying anywhere.'

'Sorry, you're right. I just... I haven't met many
people who haven't flown before.'

'Yeah well, enough trying to divert attention
back onto me. This is about you.'

'I wasn't. Though you must know enough about
the UK to know it's not known for the sun.'

'But you have coastal towns. I've seen them
on the TV. And people surf over there. I met a
guy in the bar just recently who said he learned
in some place where the land ends.'

'You mean Land's End.'

'That's what I said.'

'No, that's what it's called. Land's End. It's in
the south of England. A pretty place at the tip of
the southwestern peninsula.'

'Well, whatever, it was there that he learned.'

'Yes, well, good for him. I'm not ashamed to
admit that I'm a fair-weather surfer and I prefer my sea a few degrees warmer than the biting
temps of the Atlantic. And no matter how beautiful Land's End is when the sun is shining, it's
too rare an occasion for me.'

'So you can't take the cold, fair enough.'

'You also drive on the right side of the road.'

She cocked her head. 'We drive on the left.'

He gave her a lopsided grin and damn if a
sharp frisson of excitement didn't rush through
her middle...

'That's what I said—the *correct* side.'

She laughed trying to quash the rush within her as she prodded him with her index finger. 'Funny!' Though the sound warbled out of her as her body reacted to the contact. A second at most where the tip of her finger pressed into the solid wall of his chest, and that was all it took for his heat to burn through her. For the hint of his strength to make her palm tingle with the desire to explore the rest of him. She curled her fingers into a fist, snatched it back. Not going to happen!

Just because he's not a beach bum, or a judgemental snob, it doesn't mean you can get the hots for him. You're here to get your life on track, not derail it with a holiday fling.

Especially with someone way out of your league. On a different life track entirely.

'Oh, the joy of the English language,' she said hurriedly, picking up her pace. 'With all its peculiarities and double entendres.'

'You see, that's another benefit.'

'What is?' Now she was confused. What had they been talking about? Oh, yes, Australia and why he'd chosen to buy a place here.

'Not having to learn another language.'

'I feel like this is all surface-level stuff.'

Her eyes tracked Precious in the sea as she waved her hand through the air under the pretence of waving off his reasoning when she was still trying to wave off the lingering effect of *him*.

'Surface level?'

'Sure.'

She tugged her phone from her pocket, took some snaps of Precious to send to Sasha later... along with the truth about their companions. She was sure once Sasha knew how adorable Ralph was—and how kind Rick was—her sister would be more than happy that they'd all become acquainted.

Fae could hope.

'Can't one move country for surface-level stuff?'

'Halfway across the world?'

She pocketed her phone and shoved her glasses into her hair, turned to walk backwards before him. Maintaining a safe distance, she brazenly studied him and the enigma he represented. The image didn't fit with the upper-crust accent, but it *did* fit with the surroundings. The van. The life he was now living. Very much so.

Was he working to fit in, or *was* this him?

Had she judged him wrong from the moment he had spoken?

You already know the answer to that.

But still, the accent... His life before he came here...it had to have been quite different, didn't it? She wanted to know, but did he want to tell her? She got the impression he was holding back on purpose. As was his right. His life was his own after all. But she had warned him there would be questions and he hadn't run the other way, so...

'You know if the wind changes, your face will get stuck like that.'

'I'm sorry?' she spluttered, tugging her hair out of her mouth as a well-timed gust caught it in its path.

'Your face. The wind.' He raised his hands, eyes and mouth aghast, tongue hanging out as he froze into position.

A giggle rose up within her. 'Jeez, don't do that again. You'll scare the dogs!'

'Got you to break out of it though, didn't I?' He gave her that panty-melting lopsided grin, normal charm service resuming, and she spun away before the heat reached the apex of her thighs, where it had threatened to head all day.

What *was* it about him?

He shouldn't be her type.

No, correction. To look at, he was. To listen to, he wasn't.

Maybe that's what she had to do. Listen, not look.

And encourage your prejudicial nuances... really?

'It did,' she conceded, eyes tracking the dogs once more…as they should be.

Responsible dog walker…go, me!

'So come on, there has to be more to it, surely? I know of people who upped and left the UK for Australia to follow their careers, their family, a loved one... Is that what it was—did you meet a girl, fall in love...?' She waggled her brows.

'God, no.' This time his chuckle was tight, stilted. 'Only a fool would move for love.'

'Yet people do it all the time.' She folded her arms, pressed her lips together, thought of the people who had come to her bar to drown their sorrows after such extreme moves had gone disastrously wrong.

'Not you though?'

He could tell all that by her voice...

'No, not me.'

'Not a fan either?'

She flicked him a look. 'Of love?'

He nodded, the crease between his brows just visible behind his shades.

'Don't trust it. Don't want it. Don't believe in it. Actually...' She paused, thinking about it further with the recent developments in her life. 'That's not *quite* true.'

'No?'

'I believe it's possible for some people. Or at least, I hope it's possible.'

'Because of your mother?'

'Yes. And Sasha. She married her BFF last week. Who'd have thought it? Known each other for years and years then one day, poof! You see each other in a different light.'

He clenched his teeth together, glanced away.

'You okay?'

'Yeah. Just stood on a pebble.' He flicked his foot out, shook it off. 'So she's on her honeymoon then?'

'Yup. Yachting it around the Caribbean. And they seem happy. More than happy. And I want that for them. I really do.' Horrified at the wistful turn her voice had taken, she was quick to add, 'But I'm quite happy without it in my life, thank you very much.'

'You and me both.'

They shared a look, a smile of sorts, an understanding perhaps…or was that just the sun going to her head and the alien current that he had stirred up within her that she couldn't seem to shake? The idea that maybe she was missing out on something. Something that he could perhaps deliver on…

And then what, Fae? Really?

'So not a girl—' she went back to flapping her hands about as though deliberating it '—and you've already said you can work anywhere. What about family? Where are they?'

Because she realized he hadn't mentioned them.

'They're back in the UK.'

'Mother, father, sisters, brothers…?'

'My father is dead and—'

She halted in her tracks, her feet sinking into the wet sand. 'I'm so sorry.'

But he was off, hardly breaking step or breath

to say, 'It's fine. It was a decade ago and believe me, the world is a better place without him in it.'

She hurried to catch him up while she wrestled with this snippet. It sounded strange to hear him be so blasé about it. Unfeeling, even.

Maybe it was because he was so genial. And kind. And nice about...well, everything.

'I've shocked you?'

'No.' She blurted and bit her cheek at her blatant lie. 'I mean, yes, kind of...'

'Did you ever know your father?'

Doubly shocked as he turned the focus back on her, she floundered for a beat. She could fall back on the lie of her youth—tell him he was dead. It had served her well for a long time. But she wasn't the schoolgirl she'd once been, making excuses for the man who'd never been there because he'd been too busy with his other family. His real family. The ones that truly mattered to him.

'I knew *of* him,' she said carefully. 'And he didn't want to know me. That's all I needed to know.'

And now he was looking at her, his eyes probing behind the shades. So many questions were forming...so much rising up within her too that she'd kept buried for years.

'Why do you ask?' she countered.

'I guess because it was cruel of me to say such a thing when it might have been a trigger for you, a reminder of something tragic in your past.'

She shook her head. 'No, nothing tragic.'

Not for her at any rate. Her mother though—her heart had finally healed with Tim, but it had been a long and torturous road.

As for Fae, she'd learned that some mistakes were lifelong.

Like her.

'So, what about your mum?' she said before the pain of it could take hold. 'What's she like?'

The warmth of his smile beat back the sudden chill trying to consume her.

'Ah, now in the mother stakes, I have been very lucky. She is the most loving, caring, endearing woman. Too much at times. Even now, with her living in the UK, thousands of miles away, she's doing her best to interfere in my life.'

'But let me guess, she's only doing it because she knows what's best for you.'

'You sound like we have that common too.'

'Oh, yes!'

'Because they love us dearly.'

'Very much so.'

Though her smile in return wavered as she realized that was how it *had* been. For years, her mother had been on at her. Overbearing, fussing... then she'd met Tim, and the reins had gradually slackened.

At first it had been a relief. Not to have to account for every minute of the day. To panic when she was late home and race back. Now she actually *missed* having someone to race back for.

And Fae couldn't help thinking that her mother's interference these days stemmed more from maternal guilt that she was no longer around. That she was off living her best life, while Fae was still living their old life…

Or not, now that the bar and the flat were out of the picture.

And all her mother's worries centred around the future and what Fae would do with it. Make of it. And heaven forbid, she would do it alone.

'Oh, God, I think it's happened!'

He looked at her in abject horror and she froze, the blood draining from her face. 'What? What's happened?'

'Your face, I think it's really stuck!'

'Rick!' She punched him this time, right in the bicep as the blood returned to her cheeks in a rush. 'You scared the life out of me.'

'To be frank, you already looked like the life had been sucked out of you. Where'd you go?'

'I was thinking about overbearing mothers.'

'Yours is really that bad?'

'*Was* that bad. These days she's too busy living the life of Riley with Tim to worry about me in that way.' She winced. 'Actually, that's not quite fair. She does worry, just not about the same stuff. What used to be concern about the present has

turned into worry about the future and who I plan
to share it with.'

'Our mothers should share a pot of tea some-
time. They'd get on like a house on fire.'

'Yours too?'

'My mother, my grandmother *and* my sister.'

She shuddered. '*All* the women.'

'And plenty enough women for one man, I can
assure you.'

She leaned in with a raised brow. 'No brother
to share the burden?'

'No, no brothers.'

'Then has your sister met her perfect match
and set a fine example for you to now follow?'

'Not yet.' He frowned. 'But I have a feeling that
call will come soon enough. She's determined to
find herself a man worthy of the family name.'

'Won't she take the guy's name?'

'Absolutely not. She's determined to be the first
of our line to break with tradition.'

The first of our line... He sounded so gentri-
fied and she had to bite back a giggle.

'Well, I like her already.'

'I think you would, though woe betide the man
she chooses, because he'll have me to answer to.'

'Woe betide indeed...' Now she giggled. She
couldn't help it, but it was more in adoration of
his fierce protectiveness than the fancy old English phrase. 'But for now you can count yourself
apart and very lucky indeed because since Sasha

got herself engaged and of course, with the wedding, all I've had is, "Just look at how happy she is, how settled… You could have all of that too if you simply opened your heart to it and found someone to share your life with".'

'Because it's so simple.'

'Precisely. You'd think my mother would be more concerned about where I'm going to live and work now the flat and bar are nothing more than rubble. But no, it's all about my love life and why I can't be more like Sasha.'

Didn't Mum realize how much it stung? How much it made her feel inadequate again? Just like her own father had done for all those years when he'd chosen her half siblings over her.

'But you like her? Your sister? Sorry. *Step*sister.'

She gave him a meek smile. 'Just sister's fine. In fact, if you ever speak to Sasha about me, she'll insist. It's only me that gets all weird about it.'

'Why is that?'

'It's a long story.'

'I've got time.'

'Well, I haven't got the words. Not right now.'

He studied her intently, demanding more, but she couldn't. Just couldn't. Those wounds were buried so deep it would take more than just a chill-out session in the sun to dredge them up. It would mean talking about Dad's second family. Her insecurities. Being classified as unwanted, the mistake, not good enough. A label she'd learned to live with, but to talk about it…

To air it with a guy who was so confident and sure, so good-looking, too… No, just no.

'If you ever change your mind…' He eased back and her shoulders eased with him. 'Though it does sound like your mum's current priorities are a little off…'

'A *little*?'

'Okay, a lot. But I guess she thinks a partner will fill the hole that she left behind and has more chance of making you happy.'

'Yeah, well, I don't need a partner to make my life complete. To make me happy. Or heaven forbid, define me and the person I am now. What I need is a new home and a new career.'

'You'll hear no argument from me.'

She smiled at him. 'Thank you.'

'And frankly, I'm impressed.' He paused, making her stop too. 'Plenty of people in your position would have packed up and followed their mother. Taken the easy road and benefited from their stepfather's wealth. I assume they would have welcomed you with open arms.'

Her eyes widened. He *saw* that. She shrugged. 'That's her life, her love, her road. I need to find my own way.'

'And it's admirable.'

Her breath caught. The intensity in his voice,

the closeness of those lips that had delivered such praise...

He lifted his aviators into his hair. 'You do know that, don't you, Fae?'

She licked her lips, struggling to find her voice amid the desire and emotion rising up her throat. 'I guess.'

Neither of them moved on. The sea breeze whipped her hair into her eyes but she found herself immobilized by him. His blazing blues dipped to her lips as his own slowly parted.

'You should more than guess.' He reached out to smooth her hair behind her ears. 'You should know it.'

The only thing she knew in that moment was that she wanted him to kiss her. Badly. But she wasn't about to tell him, was she?

Precious came bounding up, water spraying them head to toe and Fae leapt back with a squeal. What timing!

Precious dropped the ball at their feet and looked up at Rick. Barked. Fae gave a tight laugh.

'Do you think she's sexist and assumes you're a better thrower than me?' she said, avoiding his eye.

'You can have it if you want.'

'With all that slobber and sand?' She pulled a face. 'No, thanks! You've got it handled.'

He grinned and threw the ball far, watched as

Ralph and Precious raced off to fetch it. 'So you think she's as caught up in looks as you?'

Heat bloomed in her cheeks as her gaze snapped to his. 'Who said I was caught up in your looks?'

'I didn't.' His grin twisted, curiosity turning into something deeper, something richer as she realized her mistake and all she had given away. 'I said "looks" in general. It was you who made it about me.'

He's got you there...

'You tricked me!'

'I don't believe I did.' Rick's pulse raced, hot with her unwitting confession… So she did fancy him…at least, that's what her response suggested.

'You know I was just starting to like you,' she muttered, doing everything to avoid his eye, even picking up the ball that Ralph returned before Rick could get to it and giving it an impressive throw. 'And then your ego had to step in like that.'

'*My* ego?'

'Yes!'

'I was merely pointing out your prejudicial tendencies so that we could—'

'Oh, no, you don't!' She speared him with her gaze. 'We were supposed to be talking about you, not me. Yet you seem to have a knack for turning the conversation back on me. Turning me into some kind of faulty slot machine!'

'A *faulty slot machine*? I'm not sure I follow.'

'The kind that loses all the money while you give it so little.'

He gave a slow nod. 'Right. I got you. I think.'

'That's just it, you do. Or at least, you know more about me than I do you.'

She wasn't wrong, not entirely; he *was* skilled at talking around his past and pushing the focus back onto others, gleaning what he could while giving little away.

'Isn't that the whole point of conversation though?' he hedged. 'To share information, a bit of to and fro?'

'In my experience, people tell me their stories and I do the listening, not the other way around.'

'Well, in my experience, I tell no one my stories because they end up front-page news.'

She huffed as she raced ahead, clearly eager to keep some distance between them. 'You're funny.'

Only he wasn't laughing, and she slowed her pace to look back at him.

'You *are* joking, right?'

It came out strained, her brows drawing together.

'Rick'

'I only wish I was.'

And he knew with absolute certainty that she wasn't going to like this. He'd only said what he had to distract her from her embarrassment. Now he was going to have to explain himself.

He cursed his big mouth, because he was sure

they'd been getting somewhere. Somewhere good, a point where he sensed she was starting to like him.

And he *wanted* her to like him.

She opened her mouth and he shouted, 'Ralph!' to beckon his dog back from the outer reaches of the waves. Though Ralph wasn't all that far away. He just wanted his four-legged friend closer as he sensed the storm about to strike. 'Here, boy!'

Fae checked Precious too before her narrowed gaze returned to him. 'Rick?'

'No. Sadly, I'm not joking.'

'But why would the press be interested in you? What is it you do for them to want to know about it?'

'You know how the British tabloids are…' He tried to shrug it off.

'No, that's just it, I don't.'

Though she was probably coming up with a thousand scenarios now, each one worse than the last.

'Anything and everything is newsworthy when it comes to me and my family. Financial, charitable, royal or salacious, there's always an outlet for it.'

'Royal?' she squeaked.

He was surprised she hadn't focused on the salacious…not that there'd been an awful lot of that in recent years. None of it true at any rate.

'Rick?'

'I'm a Pennington, Fae.'

Like that's going to explain anything to her!

Her frown deepened, her glossy pink mouth forming a full-on pout, and he adored her for it. 'A *what*?'

'A Pennington.' He stood taller, shoulders back— an affliction of his youth. 'Lord Cedric Alexander Pennington, if one wants to be exact about it.'

And now she wasn't pouting; she was pursing her lips around an eruption. Her cheeks were fit to burst, her eyes dancing bright.

'Not the reaction I was expecting,' he mused, his shoulders drooping as he ran a hand over his stubble. If she didn't breathe soon, he feared he'd have to pop her. 'Fae?'

'*Cedric?*' she blurted.

'Yes.' And damn, if he was starting to feel a little affronted. 'But my friends call me Rick.'

'Good job too.'

'Is it really so funny?'

'I've never met a Cedric before.'

'And *that's* what you're taking issue with...not the title?'

'Holy sh—' She gave a cough-cum-choke. 'A lord! You're *really* a lord!'

'All right, all right, keep your knickers on.'

'You don't get to say that to me.' She shook her head, almost dislodging her glasses from her pale pink hair as she stared up at him.

'You said it to me earlier.'

'About flying in an airplane! This is totally different.'

'How is it different?'

'Because this *is* shocking!'

'It really isn't.'

'It so is!'

'It's so not.'

'It so is!'

He had the insane idea of kissing her to end the ricocheting and promptly quashed it.

'You're not winding me up, are you?'

'Sadly not.'

'So you're as posh as they come? Like a lord of a manor with land and a lady and stuff?'

'I have an estate back in England if that's what you mean. But no Lady Pennington other than my mother, who still holds that title.'

'So when you said about your sister earlier being the first of your line, you really did mean a *line* line?'

'You make it sound like a washing line.'

She laughed, shook her head. But at least she looked more amused than horrified.

'Look, Fae, I'm still the same guy who brought you here in Wanda.' He stopped walking and held his palms out, pleading with her to see he meant every word. 'The same guy with dreams of trading the concrete jungle for the open road for a month or two or three. Who wants to master the surfboard and learn to chill. And not take himself so seriously. I haven't changed because of who I know, who my parents are or who I am on paper.'

'Right.' She choked on a laugh and continued walking. 'Just a guy.'

'Fae!'

He had to fight the urge to make her stop as he caught her up. Worse still, he had to fight the urge to make her stop so that he could kiss her deeply because he had a feeling it would dislodge every misconception she had and make her think only of the connection he swore was there, burning just beneath the surface.

'I really am just a guy.'

'This is crazy,' she murmured.

'Is it though?'

'Yes!'

'Why?'

'Because...because I don't hang around with people who have titles and know the king!'

'I didn't say I know the king.'

'You know what I mean.'

'I do. And I hate to break this to you, Fae, but you do now. You. Me.' He twirled a finger to encapsulate what they were doing. 'Hanging out, but if you're having a rubbish time, I can take you back right now.'

She stopped. He stopped. And they stared at one another. For a long moment the world seemed to fall away, all he saw was her...those vibrant eyes, the quick-fire lips, the sparkly little nose ring and pixie-like hair.

Maybe it was because she was so different. So very different to all the women in his acquaintance...

'Is it really so bad?'

'Is what so bad?' Her voice had softened, taken on a husky edge, much like his own.

'Hanging out with a lord?'

'Is that your ego asking?'

'Does it really matter?'

'I guess not.'

'You guess not, it doesn't matter? Or you guess not, it's not so bad?'

'I'll leave you to work it out.'

He chuckled. 'You're really hard work—you know that, right?'

She tilted her head, her golden eyes sparkling in their intensity as they remained locked with his own. 'Is that why you're looking at me like that?'

'Like what?'

'All goofy and if you really must know, like Ralph. All you need to do is let your tongue hang out again and you'll have mastered it.'

'Wow...' he drawled, palms itching to reach for her, his body warming with the desire to lean that bit closer.

'Well, you asked.'

'And you didn't feel the need to sugar-coat it?'

'I never sugar-coat anything.'

Something else he liked about her. He'd had enough sugar-coating of the truth in recent years, when the money had started rolling back in and the women had come flocking, Zara included. Then there were the prospective business partners and employees keen to impress.

'Jeez! No need to scowl about it.' And then she reached up on tiptoes, palms hooked on his shoulders as her mouth drew level with his and she blew a gust of air over his face.

'What are you *doing*?' He laughed and choked at the same time, surprise and desire a heated rush within as he gripped her by the hips. He wasn't sure if he was trying to steady her or himself.

'I was seeing if your face would stay like it.'

He chuckled harder, tighter, stared into her eyes, which were almost level with his as he held her there. Her denim shorts and bare skin warm in his palms. Tantalizingly soft. 'But for the record, I wasn't scowling at you. I was admiring you all over again.'

'You were?' He felt a tremor run through her, the vibration feeding into him.

He nodded. 'Promise me something, Fae.'

She licked her lips, the hint of tongue adding fuel to the fire building within him.

'I'm not sure you've earned a promise from me yet.'

He smiled, because of course she wouldn't just hand one over…this was Fae.

'But I'll consider it…if you tell me what it is.'

'Okay.' His chest warmed, liking this offer and liking her even more for it. 'Don't ever change. Not for anyone or anything.'

He didn't think she was capable of surprising him any further. He was wrong. First, she gave him tears, the corners of her eyes glistening and sending his gut rolling with guilt. And then she kissed him.

Not the mindless, illicit kind he'd been toying with but equally heart-stopping as she swept her lips against his cheek and whispered beside his ear. 'Now *that* I can do. Thank you.'

She dropped back, escaping his hold, and he was too stunned to do anything but let her go. 'What for?'

She grinned wide and wiped her face clear of the emotion that had been there seconds before. No more tears. Though there had been. He was sure of it.

'Just thank you. Now shall we…?'

She started to head away from him, but he caught her hand in his and tugged her back. She came willingly, so willingly that her body was pressed up against his in a beat, and rather than let her go, he held her as he pressed, 'Then what was with the tears?'

'I was being silly.'

'I thought you didn't sugar-coat stuff.'

'That's not sugar-coating—that's being honest.'

'There's nothing silly about the kind of pain that causes you to cry.'

'Who said I was in pain?'

He frowned.

'You made me happy, Rick.' She held his gaze as she said it and he knew she spoke the truth. 'Granted, it was for a moment because if you knew me for longer than twenty-four hours, I'm sure my lack of sugar-coating would start to grate and you'd beg me to take my promise back, but—'

'No buts, Fae. I meant what I said.'

'Uh-huh, so you say.'

'I do say.'

'Uh-huh.'

'Less of the hesitant *uh-huh* and more of the definite *mm-hmm*, okay.'

'Mm-hmm.'

'Mm-hmm!'

And they really had to stop making that sound because each time they did it their chests vibrated against one another, provoking one another's nerve endings, stimulating one another's— He cursed and she giggled, which was even worse.

It really was time to get out of the sun.

'Though I am thinking we should head back. Even with the sea, the sun can be a bit much for them...and for us.'

Because of course it was the sun's fault his libido was threatening to take over.

'You're right.' She grimaced. 'I have a feeling I already look like a lobster.'

A very hot, very appealing, very kissable lobster if there ever was such a thing.

'Rick?' she said when neither of them moved.

'Yes?'

'We have an audience.'

She gestured with her eyes to hip level and he looked down. Sure enough, two dogs sat panting up at them. A sure sign they were hot and thirsty and ready to bail on the beach. Either that or they were curious to see what happened next.

And they weren't alone in that thought...

'Beer back at mine?'

But it was one thing to acknowledge he was attracted to her and her to him. Another to act on it knowing there could be no future in it. But agreeing there was no future and *then* acting on it... Now therein lay a future of enticing possibility.

She nipped her lip, the sparkle in her eyes deepening. 'What you're really desperate to ask us round for is that barbie...'

'How did you guess?'

'I can read you like an open book.'

God, he hoped not.

'In that case, fancy some shrimp?'

This time she pulled out of his embrace to stroke Precious's damp curls back from her eyes. 'What do you say, darl? You up for some?'

Precious gave a resounding bark.

'I think that's a yes.'

And damn if he didn't fist pump the air like a teen.

Oh, if Geoffrey or Kate could see him now. They'd either be overjoyed or deeply disturbed. Probably a little bit of both. Much like Rick himself...

CHAPTER FIVE

WATCHING RICK COOK was a thrill.

Watching him eat finger-licking food, more thrilling still.

And now that they were fed, watered, dogs included, they were enjoying the late-afternoon sun in his equally thrilling rear garden. She'd thought Sasha's pool terrace had been a delight, but it had nothing on this.

Black lava stone and vibrant green plants created a mini-oasis that if she hadn't seen it with her own eyes, she wouldn't have thought it could exist here in Bondi.

She particularly adored the waterfall-fed pool, easy on both the eye and ear. Its shape was perfect for swimming lengths, while just around the corner, set back and surrounded by paradise, was a hot tub crying out to be used.

'You have Bali in your backyard.'

He chuckled as he handed her a fresh coldie.

'I can't take credit for any of it,' he said as he reclined on the low-slung seat beside her—though it was more king-size cabana than seat. But thinking of it as a seat was far safer.

And it was entirely the dogs' fault they'd ended up here as their furry counterparts had taken up the entirety of the corner sofa arrangement across the way.

'It was like this when I bought it and I have no desire to change it.'

She smiled into his eyes. 'Why would you when it's perfect just the way it is?'

Her innards winced. Did it *have* to sound like she was talking about him and his face? Which incidentally *was* perfect. From his captivating gaze to his chiselled jawline, to his strong nose and supremely kissable lips—

Jeez, don't look at his lips!

She lifted the bottle to her own and promptly gulped. Though maybe she should stop with the drink. Sun and alcohol, never a good mix when her body was all too willing to get drunk on him.

'I'm glad you like it.'

Oh, she did...she liked it all. The garden. The house. *Him.* A little *too* much. Especially when she was so out of her depth. He was out of her depth—*league.* Especially when he said things like 'Don't ever change. Not for anyone or anything.'

Such words were dangerous. They could go to your head. Make you *feel* good enough, special enough. After a lifetime of feeling the total opposite.

'Though that frown says something's not quite up to muster.'

Yes, her. She couldn't help the thought as her eyes snapped to his. 'Not at all, it really is lovely.'

'Liar. I saw that look, so out with it. I promise not to be offended.'

She cursed her wandering mind and smiled to reassure him, losing herself in the blue of his eyes that looked ever more vibrant in the shade provided by the drapes of the cabana.

She should move. They were too close like this. Their bodies stretched out beside one another. Elbows planted into the cushioned haven as they faced one another.

Well, you could return to the table, her common sense suggested, and she looked to the sensible spot now like some kind of sanctuary.

Was it too late to shift position? Would he think her weird? She could blame it on her…*what*, exactly? A dodgy hip? Yeah, right!

'Is it the beer?' He followed her line of sight, spying the wine he'd left on ice. 'Would you prefer to move on to wine?'

She gave a tight laugh. 'No, the beer is fine. Seriously, Rick, I'm fine.'

So, start acting like it again before the poor man regrets inviting you over.

'Thank you for taking us out today and for dinner. I'll have to return the favour and have you over to Sasha's, but I warn you, I'm not much of a cook.'

'No?'

She shook her head. 'I'm ashamed to say that Mum always took care of the cooking, while I was always picking up extra shifts in the bar to help out with the finances. After she left, I guess I carried that on. I'd rather be in a bar full of people...'

'Than an empty flat?'

'Exactly. And the one benefit to working in a bar is you get free tucker!' She tried to inject some enthusiasm into her voice, which had started to sound far too hollow.

'Sounds super healthy.'

She laughed. 'It may be the reason I have something of an unhealthy addiction to a schnitty.'

'To a *what*?' he spluttered, mid-swig of his beer.

'By the look on your face, I'm guessing they're very much an Aussie thing. Though technically I think they're a German thing. Not that I would know much of foreign cuisine, not having flown an' all,' she teased.

'Well, I've never come across a *schnitty* in my life, and I have travelled. But I guess I've never eaten in a place that serves up schnitties.'

'Schnitties!' She erupted as she repeated his plummy pronunciation. It might be grammatically correct but it sounded hilarious coming from him. 'Probably best you leave it that way if you want to keep that figure of yours.'

'I'm sure there are worse things to be addicted to. They don't seem to have done you much harm.' His words brought her laughter up short, the heat in his eyes as they dipped over her all the more so, and she swallowed the sudden tightness in her chest—a tightness and a heat and an inordinate desire to lean that little bit closer.

'Bob rationed me,' she blurted.

'Bob?'

'The chef.'

'Did he now?' He didn't look like he believed her. No, he looked very much like he knew she was trying to change the subject up and put out the fire that had lit between them.

She nodded anyway. 'He absolutely did. No more than once a week.'

'You really miss it, don't you?'

She swallowed the sudden lump in her throat. 'Yes.'

'Please tell me that passion isn't all about the schnitties.'

She gave a tight giggle—it was about so much in that moment. The past, the present, the confusing race of her thoughts in his presence. The fire that she desperately wanted to act on but feared more than anything.

It wasn't like she knew what she was doing either. Her experience was limited to a silly crush in high school and the odd fumble after hours in the bar.

She'd never had the time for a real relationship. Nor the inclination.

And at least with him, she was guaranteed *all* the sparks before they both moved on with their lives if this heat was anything to go by.

Though who was to say it wasn't all in *her* head, *her* body, an entirely one-sided desire. Because *look* at him—he was all godlike and she was...well, she was simply her. Ordinary.

She wasn't Sasha. She didn't turn heads. She was a nobody.

'Oh, my God, it really is all about the schnitties. I'm going to have to try one.'

'What, no!' She covered her mouth, more to hide her all-consuming blush than her beer spray as she choked on a true belly-rousing laugh. 'It's not about a good schnitty. Though once you try one of Bob's chicken schnitzels—that's what they are, you know, tenderized chicken that's been crumbed, fried and loaded up—even you would struggle not to miss it.'

He smacked his lips. 'Yum.'

'Are you mocking me and my addiction?'

'I wouldn't dare.'

His eyes danced and her fingers itched to reach out and give him a shove but—been there, got the T... Fireworks!

'I'll just have to take your word for it.'

'And you know what my word is worth.'

'I do.'

He smiled at her, the meaning in that one look causing the lump in her throat to return as she attempted a smile back. And she'd thought touching him was dangerous!

Supping her beer, she looked away before she said something—*did* something stupid. She focused on the conversation they'd been having, on what she truly did miss about her days in the bar.

'But as much as I loved the food, and Bob—Bob was fun, when he wasn't losing his cool over something in that special way that chefs do—it's the customers I really miss. Yes, the money from the extra shifts came in handy but I actually loved being there, around the people. Bringing out a smile when they'd had a day from hell. Coaching them through whatever mess life had thrown at them. Just being there and feeling like I was helping in some way, sharing their load, making a difference.'

'Have you thought about turning that into a career?'

'Which bit?'

'The talking, the being there for people? Getting paid to be a professional ear?'

She cocked a brow at him. 'A professional ear?'

'You could be a counsellor? A therapist? A life coach?'

'A life coach?' She choked. 'Look at me—what do I know about life and how to live it? I can't even get mine right.'

'But you've just told me about all those customers you think you've helped over the years by being there, or am I mistaken?'

'No, but...'

'And I get the impression you've lived through a lot in your— How old are you?'

She felt her cheeks warm. Not through shame so much as something else...something she couldn't quite put her finger on. 'Twenty-four.'

He nodded. 'Twenty-four years. I think you have a lot to give. And if that's where your passion lies, listening to others, helping them, then you shouldn't reject it out of hand.'

Why did it feel like he was lifting her up? Sitting her upon a pedestal. Encouraging her to be loud and proud of what she had achieved, rather than have her slinking away with embarrassment over what she hadn't.

'I don't know.'

'You should think about it.'

She lowered her lashes, picked at the label on her beer bottle as she considered all he had put to her. All she had admitted voluntarily and meant every word of, and how he had turned that back around and spun it in such a way as to make it into something positive, something she could use to build on. Progress with. Make a future out of.

Something that wasn't just a continuation of the old. But something new. Something exciting. Something that could help people and help herself too. A true career, a true passion, a life that was of her own making too.

'I will. Thank you.'

Because she would. Now that he had sown the seed. Because he wasn't wrong. And people went back to college at all ages. She could work and study part-time, get the necessary qualifications if that's what she wanted to do. It was an option she'd never considered before but he was right; it played to her natural talents and her passion.

He'd known her all of twenty-four hours and had figured that out.

Mind. Blown.

Bzzz... Bzzz... Bzzz...

Her blown mind snapped back together as her phone started to travel across the side table with an incoming call. She reached out to grab it. Sasha. She cursed. She'd forgotten to send her the update she'd promised.

'Everything okay?'

'Sorry, do you mind if I just…?' She gestured to the phone as the call cut off. 'It's Sasha checking in.'

'Wow, it must be the crack of dawn for her.'

'Told you, Precious is her everything. Well, her everything plus her wife.'

'Of course. You go ahead.'

Hearing her name, Precious had lifted her head and was now yawning wide as she watched them. Fae typed a quick message to Sasha, filling her in on their trip to the beach. She paused. She wanted to tell her about Rick and Ralph. But that would require a longer explanation and, in all honesty, a face-to-face chat too.

She added a quick Video chat in morn? This eve for you. And dropped in a photo of Precious on the beach, careful to make sure it only showed her furry pooch enjoying the waves.

Sasha's response was immediate and effusive, full of gushing emojis.

Perfect! Call me when you're up, we'll be around! Speak soon! Love to you and P xxx

She dropped the phone back down and Precious, sensing she wasn't about to be called upon to perform, stood, circled and flopped back down. Positioning herself that little bit closer to Ralph, who opened one eye to greet her and promptly closed it again with a satisfied grunt.

Fae smiled softly. They were so comfortable with one another and as she took in the slightly dishevelled pooch, Fae realized she too felt a little more comfortable with her. Perhaps because Precious *looked* more mongrel than pedigree hound, much like Fae herself.

And there she went being ridiculous again.

'What was that sigh about?'

'You'll think me ridiculous.'

'Try me.'

'If I tell you, you can never tell Sasha.'

'Ha, I don't think you ever need to worry about what I will or won't say in front of Sasha.'

'Really? Why's that?'

'I don't think your sister will stay in my orbit long enough to tell her anything.'

She bit her lip and looked away. Supped her beer. Oh, dear. Just how rude had Sasha been to him when they'd met? Was she *that* worried about Ralph around Precious? And if she was, what did that mean for their convo come morning?

But they were so happy together. Ralph and Precious, she meant. Perfect in fact.

So where was the harm? Truly.

'What did Sash say to you?'

'She said very little and moved very fast. Impressive really.' He grinned. 'It seems both you *and* your sister are ones for acting on first impressions and for whatever reason, I failed to pass the test.'

Her shame was written in her eyes, but she refused to look away. She had to own this for her sister as well as herself.

'Sasha's very protective of Precious. If she gave you the impression she wanted to steer clear of you, I'm sorry, but it was more about concern over her dog than anything else.'

'Concern?' He frowned. 'What did she think was going to happen?'

Her cheeks bloomed and his brows disappeared into his hairline. 'Oh, right. I see.'

He cleared his throat, his gaze drifting to the dogs safely and very innocently asleep across the way.

'In that case, consider me and Ralph very much told on that score. I'll bear it in mind when I next see her. As for what you were thinking about…?'

Oh, God, her?

She was thinking all manner of things, none of which she should be thinking but all of which she wanted. One straight after another.

'Me?' she gulped.

'The thought that triggered the sigh? The thing I can't tell Sasha.'

'Oh, right…yeah, that.'

Her blush deepened as she looked to the dogs too, reminding herself of where her head had been before everything else had taken over.

'Is it awful that I kind of like her like this?' She nodded to Precious. 'I haven't brushed her down properly yet so she's kind of scrappy. Less polished. I almost don't want to brush her down tonight and have her looking so perfect again.'

He huffed into his beer as he took a swig.

'You think she looks more like your dog.'

'More like she's on my level, yes.'

'Have you considered that maybe you put too much stock in appearances?'

Had she? Only her entire life.

But what else did she have to go on when she'd been pushed out, singled out, victimized because of her own apparent shortcomings?

'Perhaps that's easy for you to say when you come from a titled family with land, status and wealth. You didn't have to worry about appearances because you already had what everyone else wanted.'

'Until I didn't.'

And just like that the sizzle and the fun, the joy of the day, got taken out by the dark cloud that came over him.

She shivered as she lowered her beer bottle to the bed. 'Sorry, Rick, I didn't mean...'

'You did.'

'I just...'

'You felt overexposed, and wished to expose me too.'

And what could she say to that, when he was right? He knew her better than she knew herself at times. And that terrified her as much as it lured her in.

CHAPTER SIX

'MAN, YOU REALLY are insightful—you know that, don't you?'

Surprise broke through the tension that had clawed its way through every limb. A compliment was the last thing he'd expected. More defensiveness. More retaliation, yes. But a compliment…?

'Growing up in a house predominantly filled with women can do that to you.'

He'd also found his grandmother to be more emotionally intelligent than most. Whether it was through her own loss of his grandfather at a young age or living through her son's self-destruction, the woman had lived and learned and knew a lot about life. She was always willing to lend an ear or offer up advice. Though there were times when he chose not to listen…like when she jumped on the marriage bandwagon.

So I wonder what she'd make of this cosy scene right now?

He cleared his throat and thoughts in one. 'And you were the woman who likened herself to a faulty slot machine earlier today, so it was hardly a leap.'

'I did, didn't I?' She gave a small smile. 'You really do listen, don't you?'

'Always.'

And still the scales were tipped in his favour. No wonder she was on the defensive. She studied his face a moment longer and then she lowered her lashes, rolled away.

'Maybe it's time Precious and I made a move, it's—'

'It was my sister who insisted I get Ralph,' he interjected, ready to give her more. To make it fair. To make her stay…

And what was he being so cagey about anyway. It was simply the truth. He was a grumpy old bastard and he was doing his best not to be. 'Apparently I needed to get a life and she thought getting a dog would aid that.'

She dropped back, her gaze lighting up as it reconnected with his. 'Get a life? How so?'

'Settle in and I'll tell you.'

She leaned back into the cushions, her appreciative smile worth every uneasy beat of his pulse.

'Up until very recently my life revolved around work. I don't just mean Monday to Friday, daylight hours, I mean every waking moment. I was in a road traffic accident a couple of years back and while they were trying to run their tests, I kept demanding my phone be returned to me so that I could call Geoffrey—'

'Geoffrey?'

'My personal assistant. Not my mother or my sister. My PA. And not because I wanted to get word out that I was okay but because I had meetings to reschedule, emails to respond to, things that needed to be actioned that couldn't wait, not to my mind. They finally relented when they realized my heart was suffering more through lack of connection to the world than the injuries I'd sustained.'

'That's...'

'Sad, I know.'

'I was going to say *concerning*, but I guess *sad* is a good word too.'

He lowered his beer bottle to the bed and ran a hand across his neck recalling the many things he'd said and done over the years that, looking back, made him grimace now.

'You know, there's always that person at a social event—a christening, a wedding, something special where everyone's wrapped up in the emotion of it and then a phone goes off...'

'Let me guess, you?'

'I'd make a quick exit. Try and be as inconspicuous as possible, but by then it's too late, the damage is done. That's if I got to the event at all. Most of the time, I'd make my excuses up front and send a gift in my place. Though you have to understand, I don't owe these people anything. I don't have friends anymore as such. What friends I had when I was younger, I lost a decade ago, when my family became social outcasts for a spell.'

Her eyes widened. 'You were...*cast out*?'

'Oh, yes. And since then I haven't had the time or the desire to form new friendships, real friendships.'

'So that's what you meant just now...' She hesitated, her cheeks warming. 'When you said you didn't always have what everyone else wanted?'

'Yes.'

'What...what happened?'

'My father.'

He got the impression she already knew that much. She barely blinked, holding his gaze, the warmth and trust in her eyes urging him on. Making him feel secure enough to recall those days and a time before...

'When I was a kid, he was my idol. I wanted to be him in every way. People loved him, or so I thought. He was always the centre of attention, everyone wanted to be in his circle, in *our* circle... He was forever throwing his money about—fast cars, yachts, lavish parties and hotels—there seemed to be this never-ending supply of cash and while others piled on for the ride he saw no need for restraint.'

He supped at his beer, willing it to wash away the bitter taste.

'I was thirteen when I found him with a half-naked woman in his study, coke lined up on his desk. He tried to tell me it was some prank, but I was young, not stupid.'

She paled, her eyes awash with his pain. 'You must have been crushed.'

'Inside, I was crushed. But outside, everything was so normal. Mum was normal. My sister was normal. Gran and the rest the world, all normal. Oblivious to anything out of the ordinary. So I just thought maybe it's a blip. Some random act that I had the misfortune of witnessing. Not the prank Dad tried to dismiss it as, but a one-off. And I was away so much at boarding school that I could push it to the back of my mind, almost forget it had ever happened.

'And I was happy. I'd found my place amongst my peers, discovered a passion for mathematics and I was doing well. Kate was a year older than me and had never left home. In hindsight, I don't think the money had been there for both of us to go to boarding school and being the boy, and the heir, I was the one to invest in—she was not. A joke really since she was the one who lived in Dad's shadow, who by the age of eighteen could run that estate with her hands tied behind her back and her eyes closed...'

He took another drink, raked a hand through his hair.

'I figured, so long as things were okay at home, things *had* to be okay, right. Call it naivety. Childish hope. Selfish ignorance.'

'I think you're being a bit hard on yourself. You were thirteen, Rick. You did nothing wrong.'

'I was blinkered. So determined to make my own fortune in this world, to build on the Pennington name rather than take the title and the wealth that had been handed down the generations.' He gave a scoff as he realised how stupid that had been. 'But there was barely anything aside from the land left, and even that he'd started to mortgage off piece by piece. If he'd lived...'

He shook his head, not wanting to put words to the fact that his father's untimely death had saved them from total ruin.

'It turned out, it wasn't all roses at home. That Kate knew and had been protecting me, not wanting to taint my view of Dad. Mum the same. All of us protecting the other. Even poor Gran. The only person unconcerned with protecting anyone was Dad. The only person he wanted to protect was himself, and when he couldn't do that anymore, when his actions could no longer be hidden and people started to turn their backs on him, he took his own life.'

He'd never said it out loud before. And to say

it now... It hung in the air between them. Raw. Unfiltered. And finally, out there.

'Rick, I'm so sorry.' She covered her mouth, eyes glistening up at him. 'I... I can't even begin to imagine how that must have been for you. For your family.'

He took a breath, his brows lifting with surprise, a strange sense of release flowing through him. 'And I've never said that to anyone before, but it felt good just to be free of it.'

'I'm sorry I've made you relive it.'

'You haven't, you've helped me get it off my chest. Admit it to myself, I guess. The truth is, we don't know if it was intentional or accidental. He was an addict, Fae. Drink. Drugs. Sex. Gambling. You name it. He never knew when enough was enough. If only I'd taken that episode in his study at face value, I could have...'

'Could have what? You were a child—what could you have possibly done differently?'

'I don't know. Called him out for a liar, told him to get help. Told my mother. Not left my sister to live through it alone. The things she must have witnessed, the things she had to endure...'

'She could have told you.'

'She was too busy protecting me from the truth.'

'And you her. You talk about admiration for what I did but look at you. I had no choice in what I did, not really. I kind of fell into the role I played for others behind the bar. Whereas you, you had plenty of choice and yet you chose the tougher route. You chose to study hard and find a way of making your own money, rather than take what you thought was coming to you by birth and bumming off it like a thousand others would.'

'Let me guess, another of the thoughts you had about me when we met?'

She didn't need to say it; the pink in her cheeks said it for her. And one day he'd make her explain herself and her prejudice but right now it was his turn because…*slot machine.*

'Places like this are full of people like that,' she said softly, though he sensed the guilt she felt in admitting it.

'And money attracts money.'

'Yes.'

'And I have no interest in those that want to come flocking, Fae.'

'Because they are the same as those that desert you when you have none?'

'Exactly.'

'Did they really do that? Your friends?'

It was more than just his friends; it was Zara. But he saw no need to taint such a perfect evening with mention of his ex-fiancée. His father was enough.

'It started with whispers behind my back, but eventually people started to take a wide berth in public, make excuses not to meet up. Eventually

I stopped giving them the opportunity to cut me out and cut them out instead. That was when Dad was around, and when he was gone, well, my priorities shifted. I didn't have time to socialize, or to care what they thought. They didn't matter. My family and saving the estate did.'

'But knowing you like I do, I can't imagine how your friends could do that. They must have known you were hurting.'

'I had the odd friend return following Dad's funeral only to find a story printed in the tabloids soon after. I learned my lesson there.'

She cursed.

'My sentiments exactly.'

'How on earth did you get through it?'

'I had my family and they can be quite fierce. My mother never shed a tear. Not in front of me at any rate. I warrant it was a relief for her, to no longer have to turn a blind eye to Dad's behaviour.'

'And your sister?'

'In the early days, my sister spent all her time out on the land. With the gamekeeper and in the stables. Anything to avoid being in the house. Now she runs that land far better than any man, me included.'

'And your grandmother, is she your father's mother or...?'

He nodded. 'Though I think she felt she'd lost her son years before to all his vices and now we're all that's left. We're everything to her…so long as we're okay, society can take a running jump.'

'Good woman.'

'She is that. And all three of them would like you.'

She ducked her head, all coy and sweet and ever more impish. Lighting the flames within him in a beat. He'd never met a woman capable of sparking such need, a need from what had been such misery…it was, as Gran would say, remarkable.

'Still, your friends should have had your back too.'

'Says the woman who's obsessed with a world where image is everything.'

Her eyes met his, big and round. 'Well, isn't it? Look at how they treated you.'

'They were under pressure from their parents and their peers. Their relationships were being tested, and their futures were being put in jeopardy merely by association to us.'

'Are you making excuses for them now?'

'No, I'm explaining why I moved on without looking back and why I don't regret cutting ties now. I didn't have the time for it anyway. By that point, everything was in jeopardy. The estate, the funds, Dad was spiralling…and then he was gone. I was fresh out of uni, but time wasn't on my side. I needed to make money and fast.'

'You didn't have time to grieve.'

He lowered his gaze as her question struck a very deep nerve, the pain too raw to breathe. He took a second to recover, another to find his voice again.

'I guess a part of me grieved the loss of him that night in his study, so when he died, it was strange. But I didn't have time to wallow in it, no. My sister struggled enough for the two of us and I had to stay strong for her. While my mother and my grandmother faced up to the social backlash, I did what I could to rebuild our financial stability. And it wasn't just the dodgy business decisions but the family estate. What good is a title when the land that came with it has to be sold off bit by bit, though Kate came into her own then?'

'You must have been younger than me.'

'I was twenty-two, Kate twenty-three. And we had three decades of underhand dealings and mismanagement of funds to undo. It took a long time to get people to trust us again let alone deal with us. So forgive my lack of best mates and personality if you will, but *that* is the true reason I am in Australia, Fae. And the reason my dear sister insisted I get Ralph. To get a life. Happy?'

She cupped his cheek, stealing his breath with the surprising touch and the look in her eye.

'I am sorry for everything you've been through, Rick, but I am happy that it brought you here.'

To her.

Is that what she wasn't saying? Is that what

her eyes were telling him? And if so, what did that mean?

Slowly she lowered her hand to take up her bottle and he wondered if it was more for distraction, a way to pause the connection thrumming between them. The heat that was building rather than ebbing with the coolness of the night.

'Though I think the more important question is, are *you* happy?' she said softly. 'Has it worked, this extended holiday?'

'This isn't a holiday for me, Fae.'

She studied him, her lips curving around the bottle once more. She took a sip before asking, 'How can it not be? Don't lords have to return to get married and make babies and pass on their beloved titles?'

His mouth twisted to the side. 'Normally they do, yes.'

'Normally?'

'But you see, my sister loves that land and the estate, and with my blessing she runs it now and she runs it well. I'm hoping that given enough time, everyone else will see what I see.'

'And what's that?'

'That the marriage, the babies, the title, they are all my sister's dream, not mine.'

'Are you serious?'

'Why not? I told you I have no interest in love and that includes marriage and children.'

He had once and look where it had landed him. Only a fool would go there again.

'But the title?'

'What about it?'

'Are you saying you're going to pass it on to her? Is that even possible? I thought you old-fashioned English types were all about male descendants…'

'She's older than me. If she'd been born a boy, we wouldn't even be having this discussion.'

'Yes but…are you giving it up because you don't want the wife and the children or because you don't want the title?'

'Does it matter?'

She stared at him. 'I guess not.'

'And she's the one at home running the estate while I'm here heading up an investment arm. Yes, my work helps fund what is essentially a never-ending money pit. The estate is vast and old and no matter how much we try to make the land self-sufficient, those bills get bigger year on year, but *she* is the true lady of the manor and she deserves that title.'

'Have you told her this?'

'Repeatedly.'

His smile turned inward as he thought of the numerous conversations-cum-arguments over the years but he knew in his gut this was the right thing to do.

'And she's happy?'

'I think she'll believe it when she sees it.'

'And your mother, your grandmother?'

'We'll cross that bridge when the time comes. I think my mother will understand, my grandmother less so. But she will come around when she realizes I'm not trying to escape, that it's not through a lack of love for the land or my heritage, but a need to experience what else the world has to offer, to play to my strengths and let Kate play to hers.'

She shook her head. 'Are you sure you left because you wanted to and not because you thought your sister wanted it for herself?'

He gave a soft chuckle. 'Do I look like that much of a pushover?'

She studied him intently, her eyes glimmering in the soft glow from the lights that had switched on at dusk. 'No, that's just it, you don't.'

'So are you ready to admit it?'

'Admit what?'

'That I'm not the egotistical Mr Darcy you had me pegged as?'

'I already know that.'

'Are you sure about that?'

She wet her lips, nodded. 'A hundred percent.'

He searched her gaze, feeling her sincerity and wanting to act on what he saw looking back at him but knowing he couldn't. He didn't want to risk what they'd found. This ease of friendship. Something he hadn't had in so long and hadn't known he'd been missing. Until now.

He smiled. Swallowed. Dragged his eyes away to take in the dogs in the distance. To Precious and her fur, which although rinsed of the sea and sand, definitely needed the brush she had so far forgone.

'I've got to admit though…' He cleared his throat, aware of how gruff he sounded. 'It's good to know that your prejudice extends to the four-legged variety too.'

'Rick!' She shoved him.

'What? You just admitted that you—'

'I know and I'm not proud of it!'

'No, being proud *and* prejudiced would be a step too far.'

'Rick!' She moved so quick he was on his back in a heartbeat, her body pinning him down. It took them both by surprise, judging by the way she froze, her mouth mere inches from his own. 'I could…'

'You could what?' He raised a brow, his body twitching to life below the waist, his pulse racing with what she was about to say—about to *do*.

'I…' She swallowed, eyes dipping to his lips. 'You really are quite maddening, you know.'

'I think it's you who is quite maddening.'

She gave a low growl, shook her head and pushed away. Disappointment washed over him as she scurried back to sit at the foot of the bed.

'I am sorry for how I was when we met. For how I am. It's not your fault.'

'I know that,' he teased as he propped himself up on his elbows, trying to lighten the sudden tension in the air. 'I just wasn't so sure *you* knew that.'

She gave him a wry smile over her shoulder. 'And it's not even about how you look because when I first saw you...' Her blush returned tenfold, and his body fired with it. 'It's your voice. Stupid, I know! And if I'm honest, I still can't match the voice with the image.'

She waved a hand in his direction, and damn, if her coyness didn't make him want her more.

'That's because it's all part and parcel of my lifestyle change.'

He pushed himself up to sit beside her. Keen to calm his body as much as his mind, which were both getting far too out of hand.

'I'm having something of an image overhaul. The hair, the stubble...' He stroked at his chin. 'My mother's not a fan. My grandmother, however, she's surprisingly supportive of the longer hair. Apparently there's something quite regency about it.'

'Regency?' She choked on her beer. 'Okay, I think I'm going off it all of a sudden.'

'Ah, so you liked it then.'

She stiffened and coloured in one. 'I didn't say that.'

'To use your words, you thought you were going off it, which suggests you were once on it.'

He nudged her knee with his and hell, he wanted to turn into her. Wanted to roll her onto her back as she had done him, sweep her hair from her eyes and kiss the lips that she had just nervously wet, again.

'Yeah, well, don't let it go to your head.'

'I wouldn't dream of it.' Though it was soaring straight there, along with a rush of blood south…

'And I *am* sorry you know.'

Her repeated apology surprised him, and he shrugged it off, his head not quite as engaged as it should be. 'You make too many assumptions, but then I've been burned, I've lived and learned and—'

'Don't do that,' she blurted, his ill-considered response hitting a nerve. 'Don't belittle me because I'm younger than you.'

'I'm not. That came out badly and I'm sorry. What I mean is it's what we go through that makes us who we are.'

'Yeah, well take my word for it, it's what I've been through that's made me who *I* am. And I don't want to ruin this perfect day and evening by dredging up more of my imperfect past.'

Which is what he'd suspected all along. Maybe he'd hoped to coax out some of that past by saying what he'd said but there were better ways to go about it. And he'd blown it because he'd failed to think before speaking. A trait he thought he possessed in spades.

Maybe she was right about his ego after all. Her words had inflated it so much, there'd been no room for thought.

'Another night then?'

Because he for one wanted there to be another and another…

She gave him a smile that was worth a thousand more and hope rose within him.

'Sure. I'll see if I can get Bob to send me his schnitty recipe and have you over to Sasha's.'

'Now there's an offer I can't refuse.'

'You say that now. Just wait until you try my cooking.'

She could serve him charcoal on a plate and he had a feeling he'd go back for more.

So long as he didn't depend on that plate always being there, it was okay.

Because only a fool depended on another always being there.

And he wasn't that kind of fool.

Not anymore.

His father, his friends, Zara…they'd taught him that in spades.

'Consider me warned and still willing, Fae.'

'A week Friday then? Gives me time to practice in the kitchen.'

'Friday. Great.'
'A *week* next Friday.'
'That too.'

CHAPTER SEVEN

FAE ROSE WITH the sun the next morning, keen to ensure that Precious was preened and looking her best for their call with Sasha and ready for a walk straight after. *Before* it got too hot this time.

She set the laptop down on the coffee table in the front room, the perfect height for Sasha to see them both, and dialled.

'Fae-Fae!' Sasha's gloriously tanned face filled the screen, her blue eyes sparkling, golden hair billowing in the breeze as she wrapped a kimono around her bikini-clad body. 'Precious, my darling!'

Precious barked back, her tail wagging.

'Hey Sash, you look as fabulous as ever. The Caribbean clearly suits you or is that more the honeymoon?'

The familiar wriggle made itself known deep within Fae's gut, but this time it was different. Stronger.

And Fae hated that she felt it. She was happy for Sasha. Truly overjoyed for her—

Doesn't stop you being jealous, though.

But she didn't want what Sasha had with Gigi, so why was it getting worse?

'It is magical out here. The sea, the sky, the sand…'

Fae widened her grin as she wrapped her arm around Precious, bringing the pooch closer as Sasha gave a blissful sigh.

'Even the sounds of nature on the breeze…just listen.'

Her stepsister looked over the top of her phone as she went quiet, letting the island do the talking for her…

To know that someone of Sasha's wealth still found beauty in such things, no matter how many times she must have visited the Caribbean, was heart-warming. But it also made Fae wonder if it had more to do with Gigi being with her this time. The company over the locale.

Sasha's sparkling gaze returned to the screen. 'So what about you two? That photo you sent this morning…' She pressed a hand to her chest. 'Utterly adorable! Was it fun, Precious, darling? It looked fun!'

'It really was. There's so much to do here—no wonder you love Bondi so much.'

'I told you it was a great place to live. A great place to come and visit too, but you kept making excuses.'

'I know, I know, consider me told. And we're having a great time, aren't we, Precious?'

Fae turned to the pooch, who had very happily planted a paw on her thigh, and smiled, surprising herself with just how much she meant what she said. To have gone from anxious houseguest and dog sitter to this in such a short space of time.

But she knew the reason why and it was time to fess up.

'It's such a relief to hear that. I must admit, I was a little worried.'

'You were?'

Of course she was! And you knew it too!

'It wasn't that I didn't trust you, you understand, Fae-Fae. More that Precious and I are rarely apart, and I wasn't sure how she'd react... and well, I really wanted you to relax and enjoy yourself and not see it as a chore. So, the idea that you're actually having fun together is more than I could have hoped.'

Fae gave an edgy smile. 'Well, it's good that you think so because—' she took a breath '—Precious and I have a confession to make.'

'You do?'

Fae looked at Precious, who looked at her and gave a little whimper as though she could sense the mounting stress this side of the call. 'It's gotta be done, darl.'

'What's gotta be done?'

Fae stared into Precious's doleful eyes and took another breath.

'Will one of you please tell me what's going on before my wild imagination has me breaking out in hives?'

'Ooh, wild imagination, sounds exciting!' The tanned, dark-haired goddess that was Gigi came up to the screen, earning another bark from Precious. 'The hives, less so.'

Fae scrunched up her face, gave a little wave. 'Hey, Gigi.'

But Sasha was looking less than thrilled. 'Apparently, these two have a confession to make.'

'Really?' Gigi kissed her wife and settled in beside her. 'I'm all ears for this.'

Perhaps Gigi's presence would ease the fireworks, Fae hoped while she led with 'About the grey giant next door...'

'What about him?'

'His name is Ralph and he's a Great Dane and he's really rather soft and sweet and Precious is quite taken with him and I know you said to keep her away from him but I... Well, he... Well, Precious... Well, we... Well, they... Well, we kind of went to the beach together.'

'Aw, Precious went on a date?' Gigi cooed.

'Gigi, how can you say that?' Sasha exclaimed. 'And Fae, how could you *do* that? I specifically asked you not to—'

'I know, I know, but I promise you there was no

mounting of any kind!' Fae rushed to say, ignoring the unhelpful flashback of her mounting Rick as she pressed on. 'Well, not after the initial… Well no, there was some butt…' She cleared her throat, cheeks burning as Sasha's eyes widened. 'I mean, dogs say hello, right, suss each other out, all the sniffing and whatever, like they do, right, and we got past that. And then they were just sweet and happy and running about together. And I… I didn't see any harm.'

'You didn't see any *harm*?'

'Sasha, darling, cut her some slack.'

'But she promised!'

'I know I did, Sash, and I'm so sorry, it wasn't my intention, but Rick just turned up and—'

'Rick?'

Both Gigi and Sasha were looking at her now.

'Yes, Ralph's owner. He's really nice and thoughtful and if I'm honest, I was making a hash of things and he helped me out. Came to my rescue. He took us to the beach, told me what to watch out for, and we had so much fun. He made me laugh. A lot. And Precious really likes him.'

Now they were both staring at her like she'd sprouted three heads.

'She really likes Ralph too. Just to be clear. Likes them both.'

Nope. No change with the look.

'What? Why are you both looking at me like that?'

Gigi cleared her throat, looked to Sasha. 'See, darling, all is well. Precious is happy. Fae is happy. You can stop worrying.'

'You like him,' Sasha said. And it wasn't a question; it was a statement of fact.

'Well, yes. I just said that. He's nice.'

'No, you *like* like him.'

'What do you mean, I *like* like him? What are we—five?' Though she could feel the betraying colour creeping into her cheeks.

'I've never heard you gush about anyone like you just did him.'

The hairs on her neck prickled. If her heart had them, they'd be prickling too.

'So?'

'*So*, I think you have the hots for my neighbour.'

'No, I do not.' *Yes, you do*, came the inner voice. 'And even if I did, what does it matter?'

'It doesn't. I guess.'

Though it did. It mattered a lot. To Fae. To Sasha.

But at least it had distracted the latter from worrying about Precious and the company her precious Precious was keeping—so something good had come of it.

'Just…be careful, okay. He's not lived here that long. Who knows how long he's sticking around for or what his plans are. And isn't he older than you?'

She grimaced. 'Barely. He's early thirties tops.'

'Okay, he just seemed…' Sasha twirled her

wedding ring around her finger, her face creased with concern. 'I don't know, worldly, I guess.'

'And I'm not?'

'What your sister means is, just be careful, kiddo. She's in protective-big-sister mode now.'

Kiddo, ugh!

Just because they were ten years her senior, did they have to make her feel *completely* inferior and incapable?

And as far as guarding her own heart went, she was more than capable; she'd been doing it for long enough.

Though having a big sister wanting to look out for her…not a stepsister, a *big* sister. She pressed her fist into her chest to dislodge the sudden wedge. That was huge, monumental, and damn if tears weren't about to sprout.

'Don't worry, Sash, I'm not going to jump into bed with your hot next-door neighbour if that's what you're worried about.'

'I wasn't suggesting you would.'

Fae raised a brow.

'But I invited you to stay so if anything were to happen and it went south—' her stepsister gave a hapless shrug '—I wouldn't forgive myself.'

Sash wasn't the only one.

'Like Gigi says, just be careful, Fae-Fae. Please. I love you.'

Sash might 'love' her, but 'Fae-Fae' couldn't help wondering, would her stepsister be worrying so much if she considered her one of them? Wealthy and worthy of someone like Rick's affections.

Fae was pretty sure she knew the answer.

'I best go if I'm to walk this one before it gets too hot. I'll drop you some more pics soon.'

'Fae—'

'Have a good one!'

She closed the laptop, sucking in a breath as she swiped at the unshed tears.

And then the regret set in with the quiet of the room. She hadn't returned her stepsister's love— her *sister's* love. Something that was long overdue.

Precious whined—the look of judgement making a return.

'I know, darl. I know. I'll message her now.'

Because Fae's insecurities were her own cross to bear; Sasha didn't deserve her hostility.

She snatched up her mobile and typed a quick message reminding Sasha that her honeymoon was supposed to be about her and *her* love life, not her sister's, who incidentally loved her too, and hit Send.

'Right! Walkies!'

She grabbed all the necessary paraphernalia— treats, poo bags, lead—and headed out. Quick to get away from next door, with Sasha's cautionary words hanging over, her own cautionary heart racing in her chest too.

She didn't like the sea of change within. It had been one thing to envy Sasha's life. To have been wanted and loved by *both* her parents from birth. Her confidence and her grace.

But to want love and marriage? To envy that? That was new.

And that was terrifying.

And that was Rick.

She kept up a fair pace until she was a safe distance away. She wasn't breathing freely until she was free of a certain someone and then she slowed to take in the paradise that was Bondi Beach at sunrise. Picture perfect.

But no matter how beautiful it looked, it couldn't ease the anxious churn.

Sasha had been right to warn her. It was only what Fae should have been telling herself. But for some reason, hearing it from Sasha... Well, it sucked.

Because it meant there was something to it.

'And while I'm in this pickle, I'm best avoiding the jar, Precious.' The dog looked back at her, gave a whimper. 'And you can blame my mum for that crazy saying. It just means we're going to have to keep our distance if we know what's good for us.'

Another whimper.

'You saying my company isn't good enough for you?'

Oh, God, Fae, get a grip. Now you're putting words in a dog's mouth.

She hadn't put them in Sasha's though.

And her sister had totally agreed with her. Hadn't she?

But she'd promised him dinner a week Friday; how was she going to get out of that?

'Fae! Hey, Fae! Wait up!'

Oh, God. Rick!

She kept on walking. Not so much pretending she hadn't heard as unable to respond. Not while her heart tried to beat its way out of her chest. But of course, Precious had no such issue. The pooch whipped around, sending Fae spinning on the spot, and she grabbed the railing before she face-planted.

And there she'd been thinking she'd done so well getting out without running into them.

Now what? She could hardly make a break for it.

Smile, play nice. Make your excuses. Say good-bye.

'Morning.' She gave a tight smile, wishing she'd worn her shades to hide behind.

He jogged with Ralph to catch them up, his grin as easy as his stride and setting her heart alight.

That's right, blame his tantalizing smile and not your body's impossible reaction.

She turned and walked, dragging Precious, who was far too interested in showering their new arrivals in kisses and paws.

'Up earlier today, I see,' Rick commented as he came up alongside her, eyes boring into her as she kept her own pinned on the scene ahead. The two dogs now walking side-by-side. The ocean rolling to their right, waves lapping against the shore as the early-morning joggers and walkers strolled along it. And that sunrise…it was to die for.

But nothing could beat the sight of him.

That's why she refused to look.

'Only a fool makes the same mistake twice.'

'Now that is a motto to live by.'

She made a non-committal sound as she tried to keep pace with Precious. The dog's stride lengthening in line with Ralph's and threatening to pull her arm out of its socket.

'Precious.' She pulled her back and the dog simply gave her that cocked brow and carried on regardless. 'Precious, *heel.*'

Rick made a noise akin to a stifled snort. 'Who's taking who for a walk?'

'Funny, very funny.'

Especially when it was *his* dog setting the pace.

'Just an observation.'

'Well, you know what you can do with your observations.'

'Stick them where the sun don't shine.'

She smiled serenely. 'Took the words right out of my mouth.'

'You just need to show her who's boss.'

'*Precious* is a spoilt pooch.'

He had the audacity to laugh. 'Precious is

showing you who's boss when you should be showing her.'

She blew her hair out of her eyes as she puffed along. 'You're kidding, right?'

'Nope.'

'All right, Mr Know-It-All. Just how does one go about showing her that?'

'Take charge.'

'By…?'

'Stop walking.'

'Just stop?'

'Yup. You don't go anywhere until she starts to listen.'

'Then our walk will take all day.'

'Got some place else you need to be?'

'No, but you must have.'

And I really need my space from you, so…

'I'm not the one walking her.'

'That's very true, so why are you hanging out beside us?'

'Good question.'

'In that case, feel free to go about your day and we'll carry on with ours… Have a good one!'

And off she marched. Recalling the exact same farewell delivered to Sasha earlier and feeling the exact same pinch of regret as she realized she was yet again projecting and being unfair.

'But that's just it—it is a good one,' he said keeping pace with her. 'It's the perfect morning

for these two to enjoy a run around Marks Park
before off-leash hours end.'

'But…'

'But what?'

Yes, what exactly, Fae?

'Is it Sasha? Are you worried about them being
together?'

She could lie and say yes. In fact, she could
bend the truth and say yes. Use *them* in the all-
encompassing sense.

'Look, Fae…' He raked a hand through his hair.
'I really enjoyed last night…'

Oh, God, she could hear the hesitancy in his
voice, wondered where he was heading.

'Me too,' she said cautiously.

'But I sense something's shifted since then.'

'No— No shifting.'

Defensive much?

'Said the coins rolling through the slot machine…'

'Rick!'

'What?'

'You can't use my own analogy on me.'

'Why not when you're the one giving me the
cold shoulder again this morning?'

'I am not. We're walking together, aren't we?'

They carried on in a strained silence, the dogs
panting the only sound for several strides.

'Seriously, Fae, what's wrong?'

She turned and looked up at him, regretting
it immediately. Luscious heat, as confusing as it

was all-consuming, swamped her head to foot as the fluttering took off deep inside. She couldn't tell if it was nerves, desire or something more—but it was there, pumping through her blood stream, thick and fast, making it hard to breathe. To think straight.

He was *too* good-looking. *No one* should be this good-looking. And when he looked concerned like he did now, that charm was magnified. Because he cared what she thought, and that made her think wild thoughts. Crazy thoughts. Like maybe there could be something real here. Something with potential.

As if, Sasha's voice chimed with hers and a thousand others from her past. *He's miles above you on the social stratosphere, in looks, in wealth, in everything that matters. He'd choose anyone but you. Don't be a fool.*

She'd risked an unattainable crush once and it had devastated her.

As a kid, she hadn't known any better.

As an adult, she had no excuse.

'Fae, please?' He started to reach out and she took his hand to stop him, lowered it away and released it before his heat could warm her any more.

'All is good, Rick. Marks Park will be good. Come on.' She dragged her eyes from his and as they walked, she focused on their stunning surroundings once more. The sunny affluence of the beachy neighbourhood. And felt a pang for home—the safety of her inner-city suburb. Because there she would be almost a thousand kilometres away from him. 'Though I'd quite happily take the Yarra River over this any day of the week.'

'Right, stop.'

She frowned at Precious, who was finally walking at a nice sedate pace. 'But she's walking fine now.'

'And you're not.'

'What?'

'I'm sure the Yarra River is spectacular enough and that Melbourne has plenty of other amazing attractions, but that's not why you said it.'

'And what's that got to do with me walking?'

'I want you to stop and look me in the eye and tell me *you* are fine, that *we* are fine.'

'Rick, come on, don't be so…'

He placed a gentle hand on her arm, forcing her to pause. 'I'm worried about you, Fae. You weren't like this when you left last night. Not even after I spoke without thinking, and if it's that coming back between us, please give me the opportunity to clear the air again.'

'Trust me, there really is no need…' Her words trailed away as she looked up into his distraught gaze. How could she let him take the heat for this when it was all in her?

All *down* to her.

She took a breath and let it out slow.

'It's not you, Rick, it's me.'

'Oh, God,' he choked out. 'That old chestnut.'

She laughed. He was right. It was such a cliché. And it was going to take more than that if he was to believe her. She was going to have to explain herself. Which she could do...minus her feelings for him.

'Yes. But it's true. And if you're serious about walking with us, I'll explain. Though I warn you, my past ain't pretty so you best buckle up.'

Because she certainly was.

CHAPTER EIGHT

HE SMILED DOWN at her, so much emotion rising up within him, but most of all—hope. Hope that he was close to understanding her. And what was truly going on between them.

'I think I buckled in the day I met you.'

'Oh, cheers.'

'You say that like you think it's an insult.'

'Well, isn't it?'

'Not at all. I think it's fair to say it's been something of a thrilling roller-coaster ride.'

With periodic whiplash, but he wouldn't mention that. Especially as he sensed he was *this* close to unearthing the root cause.

She gave him the side-eye. 'You act like you've known me forever.'

'In a strange way, it kind of feels that way.'

Because how had he trusted her with all that he had? Family secrets. Personal struggles. Things she could now sell to the press. Was he mad? Old news was still news with the power to hurt those that he cared about when given a fresh spin.

'Time clearly flies when you're stripping your soul bare,' she murmured.

Was she talking about him, or her?

In either case, he was just relieved that she was talking *to* him again.

'I guess it does. I meant what I said though—it felt good to talk about the past with someone.' He was clinging to how it had felt the night before, how it *still* felt when he was in her company, when he let go of the doubts about trusting another with his past. 'Maybe it will help you too.'

'I very much doubt it but—' she gave him a conciliatory smile '—I'm willing to give it a go and I do owe you an explanation for being so...'

'Prickly,' he suggested.

She chuckled. 'I was going to say something far worse.'

She reached into the treat bag and gave one to Precious. Stalling or genuinely rewarding the poodle for walking nicely, he wasn't sure, but Ralph came looking for one too.

'Is it okay if he has one?'

'Of course.'

She gave Ralph a tickle and a treat, then dropped back to Rick's side. Took another moment before saying, 'I told you I knew of my father growing up...'

'You did.'

'Well, a lot of people know of my father. He's a highly sought-after surgeon who spends his days perfecting the image of the world's elite. Shocked?'

'That depends. Are you about to tell me that he knew of your existence too?'

'Oh, yes, he knew about me.' She leaned in, a wry smile on her lips. 'I was his dirty little secret. The product of an affair with his eighteen-year-old housemaid. Can you *imagine* how it would go down if the news got out? What it would do to his reputation? What it would do to his beautiful wife and his utterly divine daughters?'

He cursed.

'Precisely. So, he couldn't have that, could he? At first, he tried to insist my mother get an abortion and when she refused, he had her shipped off to the city. Set her up in a nice apartment, got her the best doctors, no expense spared. And then out I popped and from a distance he tried to control everything. Where she went, where she didn't, who she spoke to. His biggest fear was that the news would get out and his reputation would be ruined.'

'In this day and age, where affairs are ten a penny, I think it more likely he was worried about his wife and children.'

The flash of pain behind her eyes was unmissable. '*I'm* his child, too.'

'I'm sorry, I shouldn't have said that.'

'No, you're right to say it. I've had twenty-four years to get used to it—there's no need for you to apologize. He chose them. I was the mistake. The unwanted one.'

'Bloody hell, Fae, you can't see yourself like that because of his actions, because of how you were brought into this world—'

'Can't I?'

'But Fae…'

'Anyway, he insisted I was privately schooled,' she spoke over him. 'Liked to throw money at his problems. I think he was trying to assuage his guilt by making sure Mum and I never wanted for anything. Couldn't claim me, but he'd make damn sure he felt good about me any chance he got. Never spoke to me, never looked me in the face, never asked me what I wanted. And hell, I was miserable as sin at those schools. Singled out for being the weirdo who dressed differently, acted differently and, heaven forbid, had a cleaner for a mother.'

'But if your father was sending money, why couldn't you make yourself…you know…?'

'Fit in? Look the part?'

Her eyes were fire and ice, burning him to the ground.

'Because I *knew* I wasn't one of them. I didn't want his money to buy me the designer handbag that every girl was after. Or to splurge on shopping trips that were all about flexing your bank balance. Or to leave Mum for days at a time to go on the ridiculously expensive trips the school would put on. What I wanted was a father that would turn up to parents' evening or cheer me on at netball. What I wanted was a father who was there for me. What I wanted was a father who—'

She broke off. Not that she needed to finish, he was already there…

'You wanted a father that loved you.'

'Yes. I wanted a father that loved me like he clearly loved his other family.'

'You don't know what went on inside those four walls. You don't know what shape that love took.'

He doubted it was the rosy, idealistic picture she'd clearly built it up to be. Not with a man like that.

'He loved them over me. Protected them over me. Chose them over me.'

'Perhaps. But can't you see that it wasn't your fault? That it had nothing to do with who you are?'

'It doesn't matter. It's shaped who I've become and I'm sorry that you bore the brunt of it.'

'You just need to give people a chance before you go giving them this…'

He nudged her shoulder with his knuckles. 'Just because some of us are wealthy and *sound* it, it doesn't mean we're all jerks.'

She gave him a weak smile. 'I know and, believe me, I tried. Those days back in private school, I tried. I tried to get to know people, let them in, and it backfired. Spectacularly.'

She chewed her bottom lip and he fought the urge to tug the poor flesh free. To make her look at him as he told her in no uncertain terms how beautiful, how funny, how captivating she was. To encourage her to open up and trust him with it, as he had trusted her the night before.

'Oh, there was the silly stuff like getting your lunch stolen, or your clothes hidden after training. Getting picked for the team and no one throwing you the ball. Getting "bogan" stuck to your back and not realizing until you get home.'

'Bogan?'

'Not heard that one before, huh?'

He shook his head.

'Just putting me in my place, reminding me that I didn't belong. Once a westie, always a westie—I heard that a lot too. But having "bogan" stuck on my back and enduring a trail of smothered laughter all day, that was a real treat.'

He cursed, his stomach churning as she tried to make light of it.

'And then it all came to a head one day.'

'How so?'

Though he was pretty sure he didn't want to know.

'There was this guy, Jasper. *All* the girls loved Jasper.'

Not the lead-in he was expecting...or wanting.

'How old were you, just so I can get a handle on this tale?'

'Fourteen.'

No hesitation. The memory so sure in her mind, as was the damage to her soul.

He'd hoped the added detail would make him feel better. It didn't. A rush of protective heat overlaid the jealous burn, his fists clenching with his gut.

'And even though I was young, I should've known better because he was *way* out of my league. We're talking me here and him, way up there...' She flung her hand in the air. 'Good-looking. Clever. Funny.'

Her gaze flitted in his direction and away just as quickly. Whoa, what was that about?

'Pretty unbelievable, right? All the girls wanted to snog his face off, all the guys wanted to be his mate, and here he was showing an interest in me. Hanging around after class to wait for me. Wanting to carry my bag. Take me for pizza. Whatevs. At first, I was wary, couldn't believe he could possibly mean it. I told Mum about it and she was like, of course he likes you, you are beautiful and you are kind, and just as good as all those other girls. I should have known Mum would have her Mum spectacles on. But I lowered my guard, let him flatter me, and after a couple of weeks, I caved. Said yes to a date.'

She gave a mocking laugh, her cheeks colouring as she looked away.

'Turned out I was some dare. I sat in that cor-

ner booth like some loner until thirty minutes in
I overheard the sniggering. Sure enough, there
they were pressed up against the glass, pointing
and staring. It was all I could do to pay for the
single Coke I had sipped and walk out with my
head held high. Mum was traumatized, of course,
for convincing me to take a chance on him. And
I tried not to cry, for her sake, told her I was fine.
But then the bullying took on a whole new level,
social media being the toxic hell that it is, and I
couldn't hide that from her. They made memes
about me, you know. This one British lad gave
me a goatee and a bell with the tagline "Beware
of Billy". That one confused the masses, and if
you've got to explain it, it's no good, right?'

She gave another tight laugh but he wasn't
laughing; he was mad. All over a ten-year-old
twisted joke. So mad he couldn't speak through
the sickness of it.

'You see, it's Neville No-Friends, or Nigel No-
Mates, or a variation thereof, out here,' she was
explaining, thinking *that* was what really got his
goat. 'The pom called it wrong. But his blunder
was nothing compared to mine, which could never
be lived down. You can just imagine the kind of
comments that were flying about. "Can you believe
she thought he'd be into her? Has she not looked in
the mirror lately? Where does she shop—Oxfam?"
Why, yes, yes, I do—thank you very much. Not

all of us feel the need to keep up with the Joneses or stay ahead of them more like.'

She was being fiery and flippant but beneath the effervescent energy lay the wound, open and bare. The wound that she wore like armour to protect her soul from more of the same.

'Kids are cruel, Fae.'

'They are. Though I think it destroyed Mum's faith in human nature even more than it did mine. She felt so guilty for talking me into trusting him and then took it out on my father. Which, if I'm honest, I was secretly pleased about. For years I'd begged to go to a normal school, to be among my true peers, and she'd always refused, telling me he could afford the best and that I therefore deserved the best. But there she was, on the phone with him, having this blazing row, standing my ground for me.'

'Good on her.'

'Though she took it one step further than that and stood her ground for herself too. Reclaimed her own life. Told him she was done living under his thumb. That we would choose where we lived and how we lived and if he didn't like it, he could lump it.'

'Wow, after all that time?'

'It was worth having my teenage heart crushed just for that.'

'Perhaps, but no one deserves what happened to you.'

'No, but it gave Mum the kick she needed to take control of her life. I was so proud of her in that moment. I wasn't supposed to be listening, but I did the whole glass-against-the wall trick. I grinned from ear to ear when she told him if he didn't want to take an active role in my life, then he got no say in how I lived it. I think there was a part of her that hoped telling him the story of what had happened at school and delivering the ultimatum would wake him up to his behaviour. Bring out the protective father and that he would lay claim to me. Come running, so to speak.

'Of course he didn't. His solution was another school, another relocation, just as secret, just as ignored. Mum refused and told him we were done. We were selling up, taking the proceeds from the sale and didn't want to hear from him again. She threatened him with going to the press if he didn't let us go quietly and that was that.'

'Sounds like he got off lightly.'

She shrugged. 'Mum took the money from the sale of our home and put it into the flat above the bar, then saved the rest. We got a job in the bar below and worked to support ourselves. We were free of him and his influence and we were happier, so much happier.'

'Good riddance to bad rubbish.'

'Something like that.'

They reached the park and he paused, looking for the right words to convey how he felt. 'I wish

I'd been there all those years ago to defend you, to knock some sense into all those idiots at school.'

'You might have been one of them, Rick. After all, to use your words you hadn't been burned by then.'

'No, but I'd never be so cruel as to treat someone like that.'

'Who knows? We all behave differently depending on our surroundings and the company we keep.'

'And despite all of that you still turned out pretty amazing.'

She gave a surprised laugh, choked on it as she stared up at him, eyes glittering and bright. 'Have you forgotten why we're having this conversation?'

'No.'

'It's because I'm damaged, remember, and prejudiced against people like those who hurt me—wealthy people, like you.'

'Yes, but you still gave me a chance, so there's hope for you yet.'

She shook her head, bowed down to unhook Precious from her lead so that she could run off into the park. 'Maybe... Off you go, honey.'

She straightened, her eyes caught on Precious already racing away. But her hazel depths were distant and caught in the past. *God*, how he wanted to turn her into him, wrap his arms around her and kiss her until all he saw there was passion and warmth and—

His arm jolted to the left and his body went with it as a connected Ralph leapt after Precious.

'Rick!' Fae yelped as she grabbed him, just managing to stop him from hitting the deck as the Great Dane froze with a whine, his eyes and ears trained on a disappearing Precious.

Fae smothered a laugh. 'Now who's showing who who's boss?'

'I was distracted.'

'By…?'

A certain pair of hazel eyes and inviting pink lips and all the feelings you inspire in me that I'm struggling to keep a lid on.

And he wasn't about to admit to any of that.

He released Ralph from the lead and sent him off.

'Go find your girl, Ralph.' Then he added, remembering Sasha and her warnings, 'But behave.'

And maybe he should be telling himself the same, because the more he learned about Fae, the more he cared about her. And the more he cared, the more he wanted…

Taking her hand in his, he gave it a squeeze. 'Thank you for telling me, Fae.'

She looked at their entwined fingers, her own soft and then strong as she returned his grip and smiled. 'I've not scared you off then? You don't think I'm a pathetic loser with daddy issues?'

'No. I think… I think you're pretty amazing. You and your mother could have gone to the press, sold your story for the money. Hell, you could have ripped apart your father's family purely for revenge, but you're too kind and too good for that.'

She gave a huff. 'All right, all right, I don't think you need to go that far.'

She was blushing, struggling to take the compliment.

'Oh, but I do, because I don't think you hear it enough. Or accept it.'

'Yes, well, I'm still bitter and twisted and messed up, because I'm the one who struggled to adjust to Sasha and her father, struggled to welcome them in...'

'Because they're like the other family.'

'Yes. It was just Mum and me for my whole life. When my stepfather came along, with all that he had and his daughter...'

'You felt like he was taking your mother away, that she was choosing them over you like your father had?'

'Yes.' She said it so quietly, and this time he didn't hesitate as he pulled her into his arms.

'Stupid, right?' she blurted into his chest. 'I'm her blood and still...'

'It's not stupid, Fae. You can't help how you feel.'

They watched the dogs play together as he stroked her hair, and slowly he felt the tension ease from her body. He looked down as her scent lifted on the breeze, fresh and floral. Took in her choppy pink bob and remembered how confident—bristly but confident—she'd first appeared. Though he'd had his suspicions all along that she masked so much... and now he knew.

'Fae?' He hooked his finger beneath her chin, encouraged her to meet his eye. 'Don't dismiss your feelings as stupid. Own them so that you can deal with them and move on.'

She searched his gaze, her hazel depths ringed with gold from the morning sun. 'Spoken like a true tortured soul.'

'One who's doing his best to fix it.'

Seconds ticked by. The dogs raced around their legs, blissfully unaware of the charge building between their responsible adults. Or maybe they were aware and were sticking close, making sure they didn't step out of line. That they behaved.

But Rick had no desire to release her and as her palms slid up his front, the heat spread through his body like wildfire. Her eyes dipped to his lips as his did the same. Her mouth softly parted. It would be so easy to snatch the swiftest of kisses—

And ruin the emotional ground and trust you've built...?

'Ruff!' It was Ralph who came to his rescue. Followed by the same from Precious.

Fae inhaled softly as the lustful haze lifted. 'Please tell me that's a ball in your pocket?'

He choked on a laugh and broke away. 'Never leave home without one.'

Which was a little white lie but the air demanded it. And today he *did* have one. Thank heaven for furry friends.

He pulled the ball out and took her hand again. The move so natural he didn't question it. Though if he was to think about the number of times he'd held a woman's hand before, maybe he would have questioned it.

A lot.

CHAPTER NINE

'GAH!'

Fae shook off her hands, wishing she could shake off her nerves as easily.

Why had she agreed to this? Dinner at Sasha's!

Not only could she not cook but she had also invited Rick into Sasha's home, where there was no chaperone.

No one to stop things getting out of hand.

Nothing to stop the wild imaginings that had been building since the day they'd met.

It didn't matter that she knew they had no future together. That for all they had shared and grown closer, their futures weren't suddenly one and the same. But the connection—the sizzling chemistry between them—didn't care. *That* was building by the day.

And up until now they had succeeded in toeing the invisible line. Just.

They'd come close. At the beach. On his cabana. In the park. And every walk they'd taken together since.

For the past two weeks they'd managed to keep things perfectly platonic...*just*.

But now, tonight, the opportunity that would exist...

'Maybe we should dial your mum in, Precious?'

The pooch cocked her head at Fae, gave a yap.

'Yeah, my thoughts too.'

She tucked the front of her white vest top into her denim shorts and caught her lip in her teeth. Maybe she should've made more of an effort. Worn a skirt or at least something more than her everyday attire.

And why, exactly? You're not out to impress him, remember? It's not a date.

She strode up to the bedroom mirror and leaned in. Her hair was too ruffled. Her cheeks too hot. Her eyes too bright. Her lips too pink from biting.

Who needs cosmetics when they have a Rick?

She spun away and paced, wishing she had something else to do. But the table was set outside in the shade beside the pool. The wine was on ice. A couple of beer bottles too. The chicken à la Bob and salad were prepped. The nibbles were out. She'd even cleared it all with Sasha so her sister wouldn't chew her ear off if she was to spy him on the door camera that evening.

So there was nothing left to do but—

Bzzz!

She leapt as the intercom on the gate went and Precious skittered down the stairs, her nose pressed up against the glass with a bark. Fae was slower to follow, her breaths shallow as she struggled to contain the nervous flutters.

'Show time.'

She pressed the button to release the gate and walked outside to greet them.

Ralph and Precious were already running circles on the front terrace as Rick came up the steps. Fae stalled, her breath disappearing with her footfall. He wore a dark T and ripped jeans. Sexy AF.

She cocked a brow at the torn denim; mocking him surely beat drooling over him.

'Part of your new image too?'

He chuckled—low and deep—and she curled her toes into the stone floor, willing herself not to react but reacting all the same.

'They're also cooler too. Temperature-wise, I mean.'

'Right,' she drawled, turning away. 'You hungry? Because everything is pretty much good to go.'

'I'm always hungry.'

And even that simple statement had her pulse leaping and her body overheating. 'Follow me.'

She led him through to the rear patio and gestured to the table. 'Wine? Beer?'

'Wine sounds good. I brought some with me.'

Funny how she hadn't noticed the bottle before

now. Not! She reached out to take it, careful to keep her distance. 'Thank you.'

She popped it in the ice bucket and removed the one she'd opened earlier, pouring them both a glass.

'Cheers,' she murmured, offering his out to him and taking a generous sip of her own.

Her heart was racing way too fast. How was she ever going to eat if she spent the entire evening like this? In some heightened state of overdrive. Too aware of everything, and every bit of him.

'Cheers.' He took a far more modest sip by comparison, and she could sense his eyes on her, curious, probing. 'Everything okay?'

'Yup.' She nodded enthusiastically, almost sloshing her wine. 'Just nervous about dinner. I told you, I'm not a great cook. Even *with* Bob's recipe.'

'Well, don't be. I can help you if you like.'

'Absolutely not!' His brow flicked up and she forced her voice to calm. 'It'll only make me more nervous if I have an audience in the kitchen.'

'Are you sure you're not more worried about having us over knowing how Sasha feels about…' He gestured to Ralph and Precious, who were now laid out on the grass together.

She gave a soft laugh. 'I've cleared it with Sasha—you don't need to worry.'

'That's good. I meant to—' His phone started

to ring and he took it out of his pocket to cut the call. 'Sorry about that.'

'It's okay if you need to take it. I'm going to be a few minutes finishing off the chicken anyway.'

He grinned. 'You really don't want me coming anywhere near the kitchen, do you?'

She managed to return his grin. 'I really don't.'

Rick waited until Fae was out of earshot before taking a seat at the table and dialling his PA back. 'What is it, Geoffrey?'

'The fund-raising gala is two weeks today, sir. This is our attendee catch-up call. You know that call we have *every* year, on this day, to review the list of confirmed attendees and take any necessary action. It's in your diary.'

His PA sounded bemused and Rick couldn't blame him.

It wasn't so much that the annual charity gala had slipped his mind...though the call certainly had. It was more that he'd been living in a bubble since Fae had come along and he was less aware of time passing.

In fact, he didn't care for time passing. He'd only come to care for her. He went to bed thinking of her. Woke up thinking of her. Spent every moment without her thinking of when he'd next see her. And when he was with her, the world seemed to revolve around her. She was Technicolor. And everything else was monochrome.

Save for Ralph, of course. But then he was a great big grey lump…and he loved Ralph.

He didn't love Fae.

He couldn't love Fae.

It had been a fortnight. Not long enough for real feelings. But he couldn't deny that he felt something…something quite deep. And never before had he been so caught up in another.

'Sir?'

'Sorry, Geoffrey.' He raked a hand through his hair, his thoughts as shocking as the sudden rush of realization that was now working its way through him. He had feelings for Fae. 'Wow, that's come around quick.'

And he meant it in more ways than one.

'Well, don't forget you have your final fitting on Monday.'

He had forgotten, and now that he was thinking about it…

'You know, I reckon I'm going to lose the dicky bow.'

'I beg your pardon, sir.'

'The invites don't specify black tie, do they?'

'No, but you always—'

'Good. This year, I feel like being different.'

'You do?'

'Yes, Geoffrey. I do.'

'Wonderful!' If it was ever possible to *hear* someone smile… 'I'll give Alberto a heads-up. He should be with you around ten.'

'Excellent.'

'Now on to the gala...'

Geoffrey took him through the esteemed guest list, running off the big names that had confirmed and those that needed an extra nudge from Rick. There was always the odd personal call that needed to be made at this late stage. A bit of schmoozing from Rick to get people to remember their manners and RSVP. It was the reason they always scheduled a two-week countdown catch-up. To finalize the list and make those necessary calls.

It also gave them the opportunity to swap people in if need be. An empty seat wasn't just wasted headcount; it meant a potential hit to the fundraising total.

'Which brings me to the last table. It's the Hamiltons.'

'Okay. How's it looking?'

'Well, you know Sir Hamilton always has to be seen as holding court, even at events hosted by others...'

Rick's mouth twitched. He couldn't care less so long as it meant the charity received the funds that it so desperately needed. They were labelled rare diseases for a reason and underfunded because of it.

'He hasn't confirmed every attendee on his table yet.'

'Hamilton's a law unto himself. Always has been.'

'Yes, well, he's fully paid up with extra thrown in on top.'

'Of course he is.' The gala always made a show of announcing the highest fund-raising table at the end of the night, and Sir Hamilton would be sure to earn himself a head start on that honour. It was why Rick made sure guests had the opportunity to do such a thing. And if one's ego was what drove them, then far be it from him to stand in their way when it helped so many in need. 'And so long as he fills all those seats on the night, I'm happy.'

'He's never failed to before.'

'Exactly.'

'However…'

And here it came, the real cause for his PA's concern. 'Out with it, Geoffrey.'

Though he could already guess. The issue wasn't so much Sir Hamilton as it was his daughter: Zara. His ex.

'There's talk that *she* might be in attendance this year. Simon from the *Daily Tattle* dropped an article earlier this week with some suggestive comment from Zara that you'd rekindled your relationship and that she was looking forward to a public outing very soon. He closed it off with mention of the charity gala.'

He cursed.

'Would you like me to ensure she's *not* on the list?'

'What, blacklist her? I've never blacklisted anyone, and I don't plan on starting now.'

'Some people deserve it.'

'I'm not playing schoolyard games.'

'You're right, of course. Going on previous performances such a move will only make her throw her toys out of the pram, and upsetting her father probably isn't the way to go, but—'

'It's fine, Geoffrey. We're both adults. We can be civil.'

'*You* can be, yes, but that woman…' He could hear his assistant's shudder all the way down the line.

'Behave, Geoffrey.'

'Yes, sir.'

Rick's attention shifted as Fae appeared from the house with two plates. He smiled as he took her in. She was so very different to Zara. Her elfin features inspired all manner of *feelings* inside him as she smiled back, nervously ducking her head as she slid the dish before him.

Oh, he felt things all right. Lots of things. It's what he did about them now, that's what he needed to work out.

'I'll leave her on the list, but—'

'Sorry, Geoffrey, I need to go. I trust you have it all in hand, but if you need anything further for the gala, drop me an email and I'll pick it up in the morning.'

'Will do, sir. But before you go, there's just one more thing…'

'Yes?'

'There's also a rumour that Simon is making plans to head to Sydney…'

'Because of what she said?'

'I think there's more to it than that. He's been to the estate, hounding Kate.'

He stiffened. 'When?'

'Yesterday. Don't worry, he was thrown off the grounds fairly promptly.'

'Kate hasn't said anything to me.'

'She's had her hands full with that equestrian rehab centre she wants to—'

'She's not still trying to make a go of that.'

'She is and you'd do well to encourage it. You know she has had a lot of interest from—'

'Do I need to remind you whose PA you are, Geoffrey?'

'No. Sorry, sir.'

He blew out a breath, a niggle of guilt setting in. Hell, maybe Geoffrey was right. He'd been allowed to branch off, indulge his love of maths, make money from his passion. Who was to say Kate couldn't find a way of making her side passion into a money-spinner too?

And even if it didn't make money, if it helped her four-legged friends like his charity helped so many faceless people…

He could just imagine what Fae would say if

she could hear both sides of this conversation. She'd call him out for being a pig-headed hypocrite. And she'd be right.

'No apology necessary, Geoffrey, I was an arse.'

'You *were*?'

He caught Fae's eye, the sparkling laughter there too. 'I was.'

And imagined a similar sparkle and look of shock on his PA's face too and had to bite back a laugh. 'Now what was he doing at the estate?'

'I think the man is trying to write some anniversary article.'

'Anniversary of what?'

Silence.

'Geoff—?'

'It'll be ten years next month, sir.'

'Ten…' His father's death. 'Who would want to read about that?'

'I imagine it would be quite the puff piece with all you and your sister have achieved. Not what you would want to read though. And certainly not by his hand.'

No. Absolutely not. None of them would.

'I thought you'd want to know, sir.'

He schooled his features, refusing to let the storm reach Fae across the table. 'You were right to tell me.'

'I thought it best to let you know just in case he turns up in Sydney.'

'Consider me told. And well done on that guest

list. Hopefully this means we're on track to smash last year's gala total.'

'We're all working hard to see it happen. The prizes that have been secured for the sealed auction are particularly appealing. The ones you secured personally will raise a hefty sum and the raffle tickets are already selling like hot cakes.'

'Good, good… See it carries on and I'll see you at the gala in two weeks.'

'You will. Oh, and, sir? I know you said you weren't going to bring a date, but on the off chance Zara does turn up, it might work in your favour and cease the speculation if you reconsidered? You might need the protection.'

He huffed. 'Goodbye, Geoffrey.'

He cut the call with a shake of his head, eager to push all mention of Simon, his father and Zara from his mind and enjoy the moment and his much more pleasing company.

'A gala?' Fae said from across the table. 'That sounds…fancy.'

'This looks—' he eyed the dish of cheese-and-tomato-smothered crispy chicken with fries '—fancy.'

She laughed and he felt the remaining tension ease from his body.

'It looks the very opposite of fancy, but I'll take it. Help yourself to salad.'

He did as she suggested.

'So, what's this gala?'

'It's just a posh name for a party where we raise some much-needed money for the charity that I run.'

'The charity that you *run*?' She choked on some wine, her eyes narrowing. 'You never mentioned a charity.'

'It never came up.'

'But we've talked about so much...'

'And I never saw the need to drop it into conversation.'

'Never saw the need...' She was shaking her head. 'But what does it do?'

'It specializes in rare disease research. We have a centre here in Sydney. It was actually one of the reasons I relocated here.'

'Why didn't you say that when I asked you about your move?'

He didn't answer. He didn't need to.

'You thought I'd take it as you boasting?'

'There was a chance you would, yes.'

'But, Rick...'

'But what? There are plenty of bad people in this world who invest in charities, *create* charities for spurious reasons, Fae. I didn't want you to lump me in with them and give you another reason to doubt me. Especially since all it took in the beginning was my voice.'

She bit her lip. 'Will you ever let me forget it?'

'I'm sorry. I didn't bring that up to upset you, more to explain why I didn't tell you about it in the first place. It wasn't the most important thing to know about me.'

'No, then what is?'

He gave a lopsided smile. 'Probably that I'm lactose intolerant.'

She looked at the abundant cheese layer he'd been about to tuck into and recoiled. 'Rick, are you—'

'I'm kidding!'

'That's *not* funny.'

'And yet you're grinning, which hopefully means you're no longer worrying about your cooking and are actually going to eat and enjoy it with me.'

'Either that or I'm going to stick my fork in you—I haven't quite decided which.'

'Fighting talk. I like it.'

She shook her head, her eyes dazzling in their intensity. 'I almost wish I had burnt it now so I could watch you eat every last morsel.'

'How did you know I was brought up in a household that insisted on a clear plate?'

'A wild guess.'

He chuckled. 'Got any more wild guesses in there that you'd like authenticating?'

'None that are safe for the dinner table.' She coloured as soon as she said it, her gaze falling to her plate as she blurted, 'And on that note, let's eat.'

Why did he get the impression he'd just got a

glimpse of the confident, flirtatious Fae he might have seen more of in her Melbourne bar? The one at home among her peers. The one who had escaped the private school system imposed by her father and found her true home. The home she had since lost...

Was she finally truly at ease around him?

The idea had his grin building, his heart warming, his gut...

Well, his gut was doing pretty well until he got his mouth around his first forkful. At what point should he tell her that she may have used sugar instead of salt...or was a schnitty meant to be a sickly sweet, cheesy, crispy chicken strip?

It was certainly an acquired taste...quite different.

Much like his feelings.

'Is it okay?'

And *smile*. 'Mm-hmm!'

CHAPTER TEN

'Okay, you can say it.'

Rick handed her the last of the bowls to load into the dishwasher. 'Say what?'

'It was awful.'

'It was not awful. I ate everything and went back for more.'

She sniggered, pressing the back of her hand to her lips. 'You did too.'

'And you didn't eat enough of it.'

'Because I'm telling you there was something wrong with it.' She set the dishwasher going and topped up their wine glasses, handing his back to him. 'I followed Bob's instructions right down to brining the chicken first and even made his parmi topping. It should have been perfect.'

She lifted her gaze to his, spied the amusement dancing in his depths, and realised two things: one, he *knew* what she'd done wrong, and two, he was *laughing* about it. Laughing at her.

She raised her glass ever so slowly above his head...

'Fae, what are you doing?'

'You have five seconds to tell me, or you'll be wearing this.'

'You wouldn't dare.'

'Wanna bet?'

'Sugar!'

'Now isn't the time for your plummy swear words, Rick.'

'No, *sugar* was the problem! I think you need to check your salt pot because whatever you were seasoning it with tasted an awful lot sweet and awful less savoury.'

She frowned. She couldn't have. Surely.

She crossed the kitchen and swapped her wine for the fancy glass jar adorned with a cluster of shells and stared at the *salt* inside.

'It has shells on! Shells mean sea and sea means salt. I know we're at the beach, but come on, who would put sugar in a jar that looks like *this*?'

He gave a hapless shrug. 'Sasha?'

Nooo. She popped the lid and dipped her pinkie inside. She knew before she sampled it, he was right.

'At least you weren't trying to ward off evil spirits with it.'

'Oh, my God!' She slapped the jar down. If only she'd found out before now, took sugar in her tea or coffee, cooked more... 'I can't believe you ate it all too.'

'A portion and a half. Taking one for the team.'

She spun to face him. 'You didn't have to do that.'

'It was actually okay, once you got accustomed to the flavour profile.'

'The *flavour profile*?'

Another shrug. 'Yeah, the sugar sort of worked with the tomatoes.'

'But not with the *cheese*!'

'I don't know, cheesecake is a thing and that's loaded with it. I reckon you should feed it back to Bob. It could be a new twist on an old classic for him.'

'The guy would think it sacrilege, defacing his recipe like that.'

'Ah well, a treat to save just for me then. And at least we don't need pudding now.'

She shook her head, still disbelieving of her own faux pas, but a smile building regardless. How could it not when faced with his good humour?

'Now, shall we enjoy the last of this wine inside or out?' he asked.

She looked to where the dogs were fast asleep on the rear terrace, but the front had the ocean and at this time of night she loved the sound of the waves breaking against the shore. You didn't need music when nature delivered on this level…

'How about we move to the front room. From

the sofa we can keep one eye on them but slide
the doors open to the view.'

'Sounds good to me.'

Just like everything else in Sasha's home, the
sofa was the height of luxury. The plush duck-
egg-blue cushions were soft enough to sleep on,
and the L-shaped arrangement was designed to
hug one corner of the room while making the
most of the view.

She tied back the soft white drapes and slid
open the doors. The sun was already low, its soft
orange glow working its magic over everything
it touched—Fae included. She breathed it in with
a sigh. She would miss this when she left. The
view. The sea. The…company.

'That was a sigh.'

She jumped. She hadn't noticed him come up
behind her. Which wasn't like her. Normally she
sensed him before she even saw him.

But then her mind had already been occupied
by him…

'To be honest, I hadn't expected to like this
place so much.' She wrapped an arm around her
middle and sipped at her wine.

'Well, *to be honest*, Bondi looks good on you.'

Her lips quirked around the glass. 'Quite the
smooth talker tonight, aren't you?'

'I'm serious, Fae. Your shoulders no longer sit
all the way up here.' He brushed a finger along
the underside of her ear—the briefest of touches,

hardly there at all, but her breath caught. Her pulse charged with a thousand volts as her body pleaded for more. 'You're glowing too. Maybe it's living on the seafront. Getting out with Precious twice a day. Or—'

'Or maybe it's you.'

It came out in a rush and she clamped her mouth shut, her eyes too. How could she have just blurted it out like that? Confessed her deepest, darkest thoughts—fears even. 'Sorry that— I didn't mean— That's not...'

She fled across the room, placed her wine glass down on the coffee table with an unsteady clink.

'What I'm trying to say is...' She rounded on him, gripping her middle tight. 'We've had a lot of fun together. And you're right, being able to talk to someone about the past has been good.'

He stepped closer with every word she said. His expression unreadable but then she couldn't look him in the eye. She was too embarrassed. Too worried about what she would see. What he would see in return.

She flopped down on the sofa, grabbed her wine and took a much bigger gulp as he eased down beside her.

'It really has been good, and I'm glad you're happier, Fae.'

Did she *say* she was happier? She was confused. Scared.

'I wouldn't go that far, but I do feel like I know

what I want from my future now.' *Kind of,* she thought, focusing on what she did know thanks to him and ignoring the uncertainties. Her confused feelings. Her fears. 'I want to help people in some way…granted I won't be able to do it on the same scale you do, *Mr Charity Owner.*'

He smiled. 'I wondered when you'd bring that back up.'

'I'm not saying it to rib you. I'm saying it because I'm… I'm impressed, Rick.'

Impressed and falling a little bit in love with you every day and I can't stop it.

'It's helped a lot of people and it will help a lot more. That's what matters.'

'Spoken like a true altruist.'

'Hardly.'

'No?'

He leaned forward to place his glass on the table and stayed hunched over. His eyes on his hands as he interlaced his fingers and rested his elbows on his knees.

'My grandfather died of a rare disease long before I was born. He left my grandmother brokenhearted and my father without a paternal role model. Who knows how different things might have been if his condition had been detected early and treated?'

And there he went, trying to save others from the same fate. An altruist through and through, even if he couldn't see it for himself.

'What did he have? Your grandfather?'

'Something known as Brugada syndrome.' He looked at her and she shook her head, she'd never heard of it.

'It stops the heart working as it should, causes sudden cardiac arrest. It affects more men than women, only five out of every ten thousand are estimated to be affected…'

'Is it hereditary?' She felt sick with the possibility, her hand reaching out to rest upon his thigh. 'Do you…?'

'No, as far as tests have shown, both my sister and I are free of the genetic mutation, though there's a chance it could skip a generation.'

'So your children…'

He nodded. 'For those nieces and nephews my sister's been promising, and our line that needs to continue, the Pennington Foundation exists.'

She considered him for a moment, cherishing the warmth of his body beneath her palm, unwilling to break away…not wanting to *ever* break away.

'Something tells me the foundation would exist regardless, in some shape or form. Brugada syndrome or not, you would have invested your wealth into something that helped others.'

'You think so?'

'I know so.'

He covered her hand upon his thigh, his impassioned blue gaze penetrating hers. 'After knowing me for all of a fortnight?'

'Yes.'

'So not only are you admitting that I'm not an egotistical Mr Darcy, you're now saying that I have a giving heart, Fae?'

She swallowed, too choked up to speak.

'Fae, are you about to cry on me?'

'No.'

'Yes, you are.'

'I am not.'

'Then what is this?' He reached out and cupped her face, swiped his thumb across her cheekbone to sweep away the betraying tear.

He's got you there. Once again.

Only this time she didn't care because she was done letting her insecurities win out. She was going to throw caution to the wind and go after what she wanted…

Live for today and not tomorrow.

Right now.

Rick couldn't bear to see the torment in her face. Couldn't bear that he had put it there with talk of the disease that plagued his family. But to bring tears to her eyes…

'It really doesn't warrant this much emotion.'

She lowered her lashes, turned her face into his hand. 'Maybe not, but you do.'

Her lips brushed against the inside of his palm, the warmth of her breath too… Why did he get the impression she was telling him more? Like before, when she'd laid the blame for her 'glow' at his door.

'Fae, is this your roundabout way of telling me that you like me? And I mean more than in the "I don't hate you anymore" sense.'

'I'm saying…'

Her lashes lifted and he couldn't breathe for the heat in her gaze.

'I'd like you to kiss me,' she whispered. 'If it's something you want too.'

'Something that I want…?' Was she seriously questioning the possibility? 'Are you mad, I—'

She stiffened, eyes flaring, cheeks burning. One minute they were as close as they could be *without* kissing; the next she was soaring away. Taking his words as rejection. No!

He grabbed her wrist and tugged her back, claimed her gasp with his kiss.

And not just any kiss. He forked his fingers into the hair that had been driving him crazy from the second he'd laid eyes on her and plundered those lips that had done the exact same. He left her in no doubt that he wanted it. That he wanted to taste her, explore her, learn every part of her…

That was the kiss he gave her.

And it burned him to his very soul.

By the time he dragged his lips away to suck in a breath and tell her his truth, he was no longer sure who had needed it more, but he needed to do it again. And again. And again.

'You have no idea how long I've wanted to do that for,' he rasped against her lips, his forehead pressed to hers.

'Really?' She blinked up at him, dazed and flushed, her breaths coming in short, harried bursts.

'You better believe it.'

'I'm not sure…' She tugged on his bottom lip with her teeth and his body pulsed. 'Maybe you should do it again just so I can be certain.'

He gave a low chuckle and swung her under him on the sofa. 'I've unleashed an animal.'

'I think it's the other way around.'

Then she kissed him as thoroughly as he had her. Her dainty tongue anything but dainty as it swept inside his mouth. Her hands too as they reached inside his T and raked along his back. The perfect pressure of her body as she wrapped her legs around him making him groan and buck against her.

God, how he wanted her.

'You smell of the sea and of the sun,' he said against her ear, his hand sweeping beneath her vest top and delighting in her silken skin.

She laughed softly. 'I bet you were good at poetry at school.'

'No.' He ran his palm along the underside of her breast, felt her skin prickling to greet his touch. 'Only math.'

'I don't believe *y*—'

She broke off on a cry as he stroked his thumb across the lace of her bra, catching her need-puckered nipple… *My God.* If she kept reacting like this, he had no chance of keeping his cool.

'The doors?' she panted, gifting them a panicked look.

'Don't worry, no one can see us up here.'

'But they can hear.'

'Not with the sound of the sea…so long as we time it right.'

He smothered her remaining concern with his kiss and the rock of his hips. It became something of a game. To tease each erogenous zone with the waves crashing on the shore… He felt like the animal he'd accused her of being. Feral. Wild. Impossible to contain.

She pulled her vest over her head, no coyness now as she pulled him back to her, her legs tight around his waist, the colour high in her cheeks and chest. The shortness to her breaths telling him how lost to their self-made waves she was.

Nature had never been more stunning.

'You are beautiful, Fae.'

She shook her head, her eyes tightly shut even as she whimpered and writhed against him.

'Don't shake your head at me.'

He leaned back, his eyes burning into her. How could she not see it?

The soft light of the room had turned her skin to gold, her rose-coloured nipples pressed eagerly through the white lace of her bra and her slender stomach dipped and flexed with every roll of her hips as she sought her release against him.

Hell, he'd never been more turned on, more hungry.

'Look at me when I tell you you are beautiful… *Please*, Fae.'

She opened her eyes. Honeyed rings, almost black, connected with his.

'I want to explore every inch of you, taste every inch of you, and worship you until you *tell me* how beautiful you are.'

Her mouth parted with a soft intake of breath.

'I don't say these words for the sake of saying them. I say it because it's true.' He buried his hand into her wild pink locks. 'I adore your hair. It was the first thing that drew me in on the camera. Then it was your eyes when I saw you in person. They're like liquid gold, enough to send a rich man mad.' He was only half teasing. 'And your nose, this piercing—' he kissed the tip '—so cute and sexy.'

She gave a lustful laugh.

'And these lips…' he traced them with the tip of his tongue, coaxing her mouth to part. 'They are entirely distracting.'

He dipped inside, the heat exploding within him as their kiss took over, their lower bodies melding together in a mindless rhythm that almost had him forgetting his purpose. But he wouldn't, he couldn't, she had to see him as he did.

He tore his mouth away, rasped along her jaw, 'And then there is your body…'

He kissed the skin beneath her ear, her throat… all the while attuned to her, every sound she made, every twitch of her body.

'Your skin is like silk…'

He followed the line of her bra with his lips, his tongue…treasured the way her breath hitched, her hands clawing at the fabric of the sofa.

'And your breasts are teasing me right now, begging me to…'

He surrounded one tantalizing nipple through the lace and her hands flung to his hair with a cry. He grazed it with his teeth, laved it with his tongue, fed her whimpers before moving onto the other. Alternating until she lost all patience with the rhythm of the sea and the tempo became her own.

'Please, Rick. Please.'

He rose up over her. 'I told you—you need to admit it.'

She dragged his T up and he threw it off, cherishing the way her eyes dipped and her mouth dropped open.

'*You're* the one who is beautiful.'

'Not what I asked for, Fae.'

She lowered her palms to his chest and his pecs flexed of their own accord.

'Then stop showing off.'

'I wasn't, that was all you.'

'So it's my fault?'

'Because my body thinks you are a goddess, Fae, like your namesake, a sweet little pixie goddess, and you've caught me up in your spirit and your spell.'

'A *pixie goddess*?' Her eyes sparkled as she gave a choked laugh. 'Okay, I'll take that. So long as you—' she took hold of his jeans and eased the button undone '—take me.'

Oh, Christ.

His hands soared to hers, halting their progress. He needed a moment. Two. One, to make this last, to make it as special for her as it was for him. And two, he had to be certain that *she* was certain. He couldn't risk regrets come morning.

'What's wrong?'

Yes, what are you doing? his body screamed while his groin strained against the zipper of his jeans. He closed his eyes. He couldn't look at her and maintain his good sense. But his head was full of her. So flushed and perfect, lips swollen, pupils pleading, white lace concealing very little…

'Rick…?'

'I want you, Fae. Badly. But I need to be sure… I don't want you to have any regrets.'

'I'm on the pill.' She pulled herself free of his grasp and rose up onto her knees to meet him. 'I'm safe and I'm always sensible.'

She thought he was referring to her past and

the regrets of her own parents. Repeating *their* mistakes. And his eyes flared open.

'I meant regrets in terms of us crossing the line.'

'I've had enough regrets for this lifetime.' She eased his zipper down, her hand slipping inside his briefs as pleasure tore through him. 'I want to live for this moment and enjoy it.'

Now *that* he could do… *God, yes.*

CHAPTER ELEVEN

FAYE WOKE TO the smell of bacon, her body deliciously sore but her head deliciously light.

Because he was still here.

He hadn't made love to her, then taken flight.

He'd stayed. And by the scent on the air he was making breakfast!

She threw back the sheets and raced to the bathroom, freshened up, tugged on some PJs and hurried downstairs.

She found him in the kitchen wearing a different T and shorts. He must have nipped home. And he'd showered too.

Now she felt a mess by comparison and considered doing an about-turn when he looked up and caught her eye.

'Morning, sleepyhead.'

'Hi.' Her cheeks warmed as his eyes dipped over her, hot with appreciation and obliterating her uncertainty. She smiled, gesturing to the sizzling pan. 'You've been busy.'

'I didn't want to wake you. You looked like you needed the sleep.'

'Well, if someone will exhaust me with their nighttime antics...'

'You weren't complaining last night.'

He strode up to her and pulled her into his embrace, the easy contact along with the recalled pleasure of the night sending a shiver of anticipation running through her.

'For the record, I'm not complaining now either.'

'In that case...' And then he kissed her, deeply, his hands reaching down to her thighs and lifting them around him. 'I think I'd rather you than food, but one needs energy, and the dogs need their walk.'

'Can't we do it all?'

He chuckled. 'You really are an animal.'

'Takes one to know one.'

He gave her another toe-curling kiss then set her down. 'Come on...'

He led her outside where he'd already laid out juice and fruit. The dogs were happily curled up together in the same place they'd been the night before.

'It's like they haven't moved.'

He smiled. 'You'd think they'd known each other forever.'

'I know that feeling.'

It was out before she'd fully considered it, but

as his eyes found hers, she realised she meant it.
She did feel that way about him. And hadn't he
said something similar too, the first time they'd
gone to Marks Park...

'Why don't you take a seat and I'll bring out
the rest.'

'I'm sure I'm supposed to be doing all of this,'
she called after him, though she did as he suggested. Pouring herself some OJ, a wistful smile
on her lips as she remembered the days when her
mum used to do this for her. How strange it felt
to have someone else do it for her now. To have
him doing it. Strange but good. Too good.

A nervous wriggle tried to work its way in and
she promptly quashed it with her OJ.

'Or are you scared about OD'ing on sugar
again?' she teased as he stepped outside. Then she
saw the plates, stacked high with waffles, bacon,
eggs—*my God*, it looked good. *He* looked good.

'Maple syrup is on the table, so the sugar rush
is yours for the taking. I'm sweet enough already.'

'That you are,' she laughed out, though she
meant every word of that too.

He set the plates down and pulled his seat
alongside her, his smile...his smile made her do
a double take. It was edged with *nerves*?

She lowered the fork she'd only just picked up.
Rick didn't do 'nervous'. And if *he* was nervous,
she was nervous.

Was this the lead up to 'I had a great time last

night but this isn't going to work as anything more than friends' chat? The reiterating 'there's no future' chat?

'What's wrong?'

'*Nothing.* Why would you think something's wrong?'

'Because I'd like to think I've got to know you pretty well and for the first time since meeting you, you're nervous. What's going on?'

'I'm not nervous.'

She cocked a brow.

'Not really, it's just…'

The smile became a grim line that had her wishing she'd left well enough alone.

'I got an email from Geoffrey during the night.'

'And?'

'It's about the gala.'

'The gala…?'

'We were waiting on the final table to confirm their list of attendees.'

'And have they?'

'Yes.'

'So that's a good thing, right?'

'Yes, in that we know where we are with the numbers and have a full house.'

'So, what's the problem?'

'One of those attendees is my ex-fiancée.'

Her mouth fell open, her heart swooping with it.

'I know I haven't—'

'Your *what*?' Her stomach was in a dancing

frenzy, her shoulders inching around her ears. Had she really heard him right? He'd been *engaged*. After all his talk of never wanting such a thing, he'd... 'I don't understand. You said—'

'I know and I'm going to explain in as quick a fashion as I can because I don't want you to think I haven't mentioned her for any reason other than the truth—Zara hasn't been a part of my life for a decade and I mean that. We grew up together, same social circles. Our families earmarked us for marriage when we were young. We were engaged when I was eighteen, more a publicity stunt by my father than a real proposal of marriage. And it soon went sour when his dodgy dealings and debauched behaviour became public knowledge. Her family disowned mine, and she disowned me.'

Her heart was racing as fast as his words.

'When I told you of my friends turning their backs on me when everything went south, she was one of them. I saw no reason to differentiate her as a special case, because Zara wasn't one. I never loved her, not really. I was infatuated as a boy, yes. But love, never. So please, don't think any more on it than that.'

She was struggling to *think* on anything as she tried to fit this revelation with the man she thought she knew. Anti-love. Anti-marriage. Anti-everything she didn't want too, but now...

'If that's the case, why are you so worried about her attending now?'

'Because when I told you there were those that returned with my success…'

'She was one of them?'

'Yes.'

'And has she made any attempt to…?' Her stomach twisted.

'Rekindle our relationship?' His eyes told her before he even confirmed it. 'I would be lying if I said she hadn't.'

'I see.'

'But as her father is one of our biggest bene-factors and she's his guest—'

'Why let them come at all after the way they treated you and your family?'

'If I cut everyone out who had something to say about my family back then I'd be depleting my charity's funds quite considerably. I'd rather take advantage of their very deep pockets and be the bigger person.'

So why the continued nerves, the edge to his voice, unless…

'You think she's coming to make a play for you?'

He shifted in his seat, cleared his throat. 'Possibly. Probably. Geoffrey has suggested I recon-sider my lack of a plus-one…'

A plus-one? A date. Of course. Her gut gave another twist.

'You want to ask my permission to take someone with you?'

'Not just any someone, Fae.' He gave her a bemused smile. 'I want to take you.'

'Huh?'

'I want you to come to the gala with me.'

'Are you *mad*?' she blurted even as her heart rejoiced. 'What do I know about galas and fancy events?'

'They're just a great big party. All you need to do is be yourself and everyone will be as enraptured as I am, I promise.'

Enraptured? Now the room was spinning along with her head and heart.

'Are you asking me to go as your friend or as your...?' She swallowed, nerves stealing her voice.

'Considering the night we just shared, I think we're a little more than friends, don't you?'

She did, but...it didn't change who she was. How out of place she would be. Didn't he need someone sophisticated, elegant, a Sasha not a Fae? Would he have asked if Geoffrey hadn't put the idea out there?

'Fae?'

'Are you asking me because you need rescuing from this woman, or are you asking me because you want me to go with you?'

He wrapped his hand around hers. 'I don't make a habit of being backed into a corner by anyone, least of all my ex-fiancée, so believe me when I tell you, I'm asking you because I want you to come with me as my date. I don't know how much clearer I can b—'

She cut off him off with her kiss as she leapt into his lap, her heart fit to burst from her chest.

She didn't care that she was nervous, terrified, treading unknown waters. Right this second, she was all about him and the fact that he wanted to take her as his equal, his partner, his *date*!

'Is that a yes?' He broke away with a breathless laugh.

'To use your words, I don't know how much clearer I can be. Of course, it's a yes.'

She had no clue what to wear but she had Sasha's wardrobe at her disposal. Her sister was taller, more statuesque, but with some heels she'd be able to make something work.

And she had two weeks to solve that problem; right now she had a man plus a sugar fix to enjoy...

And yes, the nervous wriggle still existed but it was oh so easy to mute when he looked at her like he was doing. 'You know you're supposed to salivate over the food, Rick?'

Keeping her locked in his lap, he forked up some waffle and bacon and lifted it to her lips. 'Can't I salivate over both?'

'You're full of the best ideas.'

'And don't you forget it.'

CHAPTER TWELVE

MONDAY MORNING CAME around and they were in Rick's kitchen eating breakfast having just got back from walking the dogs along the coastal path.

He looked across the black granite breakfast bar at her wearing his grey T-shirt and felt an all-consuming rush of warmth fill his chest.

'What's that smile about?' She patted the top of her head. 'Is my hair out of control again?'

'I make no secret of the fact that I love your hair out of control.'

She gave a chuckle and bit into her toast, her body bobbing on the stool, which suggested her legs were swinging underneath. Much like the dogs' tails wagged when they were happy, she was happy. And he was glad she was happy, because he was happy too.

Exceedingly so, having received another email from Geoffrey overnight confirming a certain addition to his morning appointment...and he couldn't wait to share it with her.

'So you know I have my tailor coming at ten to make any final adjustments to my suit for the gala.'

She hummed her acknowledgement.

'Well, he's bringing a friend of his. Alanna. She runs a ladies' fashion house here in Sydney and will be bringing an array of outfits for you to choose from.'

She choked over her toast, her eyes watering as she stared back at him. 'She's *what*?'

He grinned. 'Surprise!'

'Rick, I can't afford—'

'It's a gift, Fae. I'm the one who invited you so it's only fair I get to treat you.'

She picked up her orange juice, took a sip.

'But I already have a dress.'

Of all the responses he'd imagined, this hadn't been one of them.

'You do?'

She flinched. He hadn't meant to sound so surprised but…

'I wouldn't have thought you'd—'

'I'm borrowing one of Sasha's.'

She slid off the stool, his T-shirt swamping her tiny frame as she dropped what was left of her toast in the bin.

'There's really no need to borrow one. I'd like to buy you one. Like I say, it's a gift.

'She'll bring a range of accessories too,' he hurried to add when she said nothing. 'Shoes, handbags, jewellery, you can take your pick. Whatever your heart desires.'

And now he wished he'd just stop talking because with every word, her shoulders hiked higher, her skin paled further.

'Fae?'

Her mouth twitched into a smile. The kind she'd given him the day they'd met. When he'd untangled her from the dogs' leads. Not good.

'That's sweet of you. Thank you.'

'Hey, come here.' He reached out for her wrist, pulled her into his arms, kissed her lips. 'Are we okay?'

'You've just handed me your bank card for whatever my heart desires—what woman wouldn't be happy?'

You, his gut was saying, sirens blaring in his mind telling him she was only saying what she thought he wanted to hear. Though aloud he pressed on, 'So I'll send her around to you for ten?'

She nodded, gave him a chaste kiss, then tapped her thigh for Precious.

'Come on, darl, we have a fancy fashionista to prepare for. Bet you're gonna love her.'

He winced. Was Alanna in for the cold shoulder?

And he thought they'd come so far...where had he gone wrong?

Alanna was everything Fae had feared she would be.

Beautiful. Elegant. Sophisticated. Sasha would have loved her.

Where was her sister when she really needed her?

Oh, that's right, on her honeymoon having the time of her life as she should be.

But as Alanna left her a few hours later in a cloud of expensive perfume and doubt, Fae wished her sister was here.

Better still, she wished her mum *and* her sister were here.

Which was ridiculous. She was a fully grown woman, going to an incredible event for an incredible cause with an incredible man.

So why did she feel like she was *this* close to Lone Pizza Date Gate again?

Rick would never treat her that way.

The inferiority was all within her.

Even Alanna and her team had cooed over the chosen dress and Fae had to admit, there had been something about it. When she'd taken a good enough look…if you can call a quick turn and the briefest scan 'good enough'.

But she'd been too self-conscious to truly look at herself while three stunning strangers were doing the exact same.

Though she knew the grey silk taffeta gave the gown a fairylike feel that made her think of Rick and the way he saw her. The off-the-shoulder cut and corset lifted her chest and enhanced her slender waist. The flowing fabric, delicately layered and reaching all the way to the floor, possessed a hidden slit to the thigh that only became visible when she walked. It had felt so perfect, even if she herself hadn't.

And as she eyed the dress bag containing it now, she wondered if she'd made a terrible mistake. Maybe she should have stuck to her guns. Told Rick she was happier in something of Sasha's. Anything but agreeing to this, because instead of making her feel like she would fit in, which had to be his intention, she felt ever more out...

Over the next two weeks, no matter how busy things got with work, the estate, the gala, Rick always made time for their twice-daily dog walk, and they always fell into the same bed at night.

The edginess of Fae's appointment with Alanna had passed with the day. The dress itself had appeared in its dress bag and remained under wraps ever since. He'd asked if she was happy and she'd told him she was. She hadn't offered to give him a sneak peek or asked for his opinion and he hadn't wanted to push his luck so he'd left it. Though every time he saw the bag hanging on her wardrobe, he had to fight the urge to look.

He'd seen the shoes. Tall stilettos. Silver.

That was it.

And the thought of her stepping out in a gown... He imagined it was akin to seeing one's bride for the first time on her wedding day. Hell, he'd never *seen* Fae in a dress. Or would it be a suit?

He wouldn't be surprised and would be just as in awe.

'What are you thinking about?' She lifted her head from his chest.

It was late, gone midnight, another passionate lovemaking session had been followed by another and now his hand was in her hair, toying with the playful pink strands as he lost himself to his thoughts.

'How did you know I was thinking about anything?'

'I could tell by your breathing you weren't sleeping.'

He kissed the tip of her head. 'Are you going to be okay walking both Precious and Ralph tomorrow? I wouldn't leave if I didn't have to but…'

'I am more than capable of looking after two dogs, Rick.'

'It's more the walking of two dogs I'm worried about.'

'Are you saying I'm not strong enough?'

'I'm saying, Ralph alone weighs more than you. It's a legitimate concern.'

'And in case you haven't noticed, I think Ralph listens more to me than he does to you these days.'

He chuckled. 'I can't argue with that.'

'Not if you know what's good for you…' She planted her chin on his chest to meet his eye. 'Is that really what you were thinking about?'

He couldn't lie to her, not when she was looking at him like she was, naked and trusting.

'I was wondering about your dress for the gala.' He looked to the item hanging in its cream Alanna-monogrammed bag. 'That's if it is a dress…?'

'*Yes*, it's a dress!' She dug him in the ribs. 'What do you think I am, an animal?'

'We've already established the answer to that and to be fair—' he let his teasing gaze drift back to her '—plenty of women wear dinner jackets these days. It's the height of fashion…or at least it was.'

'Well, I wouldn't know.' And there was that look again, the same unease that had come over her that morning two weeks ago when he'd first mentioned Alanna and his 'surprise'.

'You're not worried about it, are you?' He held her by the chin as she tried to duck his gaze. 'Fae?'

She hesitated, her brow furrowing.

'You really don't need to be. It'll be fun and you're going to be stunning. Whatever you wear.'

She licked her lips. 'We'll see. I have a call lined up with Sasha and Gigi tomorrow and they're going to talk me through my make-up and hair.'

He cursed. 'I should have thought. I could have booked you in with a stylist. They'd come here and do all that for you. It would have taken the pressure off. Wait, let me—'

He started to reach for his phone and she pressed him back. 'No, you don't.'

'It's no trouble. Geoffrey will get straight on it. It's what all the ladies do.'

'Not me.'

He gave a perplexed smile. She couldn't be serious. The gala was a big occasion and women always got their hair and make-up done for big occasions. Didn't they?

Surely it helped alleviate the nerves too. And she had to be seriously nervous if she was disturbing Sasha and Gigi on their honeymoon. *Especially* when her and her sister hardly had a bedrock of sisterhood—though he knew that had changed quite a bit in the past month. Their calls and messages had become more and more affectionate on both sides. Which was great to see but still…

'It's okay to treat yourself once in a while.'

'I'm serious, Rick. I'm quite capable of doing it myself…with some tips and tricks from experts like Sasha and Gigi.'

'Doesn't beat having an expert actually do it and take the pressure off. You should relax and enjoy it. Enjoy being pampered. Is it the money you're worried about, because I'm paying? Money is no object, Fae. I want you to be happy.'

He sensed the tension running through her and wished he could shut this down. Shut his own mouth down. But he was so desperate to have her relax, to have her enjoy what he was capable of giving her.

'No, it's not the money.' She rolled away and slipped out of bed. 'I *want* to have that time with Sasha, it's what *sisters* do.'

'Of course, but if you change your mind...'

'What time are you setting off in the morning?'

He frowned. 'I'll likely be gone before you wake up.'

But he didn't want to talk about leaving, not when he could feel the emotional gulf building between them now. A gulf he couldn't understand.

He wished he didn't have to go into Sydney. But he had attendees flying in from across the globe who deserved the VIP treatment of a pre-event meet and greet. Something he always ran personally to express his gratitude and that of the charity's. It was also the first time the gala had been held in Australia so the pressure was on to impress and make it one to remember.

'I'll be back around five to change for the gala. The car will be here to collect us just after six.'

'Six. Got it.'

She disappeared into the bathroom and closed the door softly behind her. He stared at it long after she was gone, feeling she might as well be in another country for the distance that had formed.

It's just nerves, he told himself.

And tomorrow, she would prove to herself that she could do it and all would be well again.

Wouldn't it?

The next day, true to his word Rick was gone early. Fae hadn't been asleep when he'd kissed her forehead goodbye though. Not fully.

The night had been a restless fit of worry.

How could she have thought to say yes to any of this? A gala! Her!

It wasn't even the dressing up and looking all *fancy*. But the people. A whole room of Rick's kind of people.

It wasn't like the bar, where her customers chose to come into her domain and she could be the person who she was. No airs and graces.

This was like going back to private school. Her father's chosen schools. Walking the halls with people way out of her league and she was sick to her stomach with it.

And for all she told herself she wasn't worried about his ex-fiancée because to use Rick's words, he'd never loved her, Fae was terrified of coming face to face with the woman. Knowing that she came from his world was enough to send her inferiority complex into overdrive.

Having Precious and Ralph to look after for the day was a good distraction but that only went so far. She was hoping that Gigi and Sasha would soothe away the rest.

Even if it was more creating the perfect mask than it was curing it.

'Fae-Fae!'

She'd set the laptop up on the dressing table in her bedroom and she waved at the two sunny lovebirds as they popped onto the screen.

'Hey, Sash, Gigi!' They looked like they were cosied up in bed, sharing one giant pillow, their heads tucked together. 'Thanks for staying up late to do this with me. You sure you don't mind?'

'Mind? We wouldn't miss this for the world.'

'Hardly the kind of romantic endeavour you envisaged for your honeymoon, hey? Having to come and rescue my image via satellite?' She flapped her hands at her shower-flushed face and towel-wrapped hair.

'But this *is* romantic. You're going on a date, Fae-Fae. Your first in how long?'

She screwed her face up, trying to remember her last proper date—one that involved going out some place nice—and came up blank. It was probably the nondate that had become meme-worthy in her teens. And that really *wasn't* the thing to be thinking on right now.

Her sister winced with her. 'Clearly too long if that face is your answer.'

'Fine. But let's just get this done in the quickest time possible.'

'We will, but first champagne!'

Fae rolled her eyes but couldn't help grinning

as she lifted her own glass of ready-poured bubbles to the screen. 'Way ahead of you.'

'Great minds! Now before we make any decisions, we need to know a few details,' Sasha said as Gigi dutifully poured their drinks. 'First off location. Where is it being held?'

'Sydney Opera House.'

'Exquisite. Dress code?'

'He didn't say, though he said something about losing the dickie bow...'

'Okay, probably a dark suit, maybe a tie,' Gigi said passing a full glass to her wife.

'Thank you, darling. And lastly, but most importantly, we must see the dress. We can't choose colours without seeing the masterpiece we are to pair you with.'

'Really?'

They gave a vigorous nod, a chorus of 'Really!'

She eyed the bag like one would a trapped spider and swallowed. 'Okay.'

Setting her glass down, she wiped her palms on her robe and crossed the room.

As she unzipped the bag, her mouth quivered—a hint of a smile. The same wistful smile that had caught at her when she'd spied the fairylike fabric on Alanna's portable rail.

'Oh, my goodness, Fae-Fae!'

'It's exquisite.'

She touched her hand to the silk. 'You approve?'

'We adore!'

She smiled as she zipped the bag back up. So far so good…

And for the next hour and a half, she did as Gigi and Sasha directed. Every colour choice and stroke of the brush, until finally, Sasha gave a resounding '*Et voilà!* You are ready for your dress, Cinderella!'

'Really, Sash?! *Cinders?*'

'Sorry, Fae-Fae, it's the bubbles going to my head. You know I don't mean anything by the reference but seriously, when he sees you…'

'Are you…*crying?*'

Fae peered closer at the screen as Sasha dabbed at her eyes. 'If your mother could see you now… You wouldn't even wear a dress to our wedding.'

Fae rolled her eyes. 'Yeah, yeah, I know.'

'Are you going to put it on now so we can see?'

'Absolutely not. I have to walk the dogs before I'll risk getting in it.'

Sasha sighed. 'Putting our babies first.'

Fae smiled. 'See, told you, you could trust me.'

'Just look at them…' Sasha was all goo-goo-eyed as she looked past Fae to the two dogs, who had appeared halfway through the makeover session and curled up together on Fae's bed. 'They're so sweet together.'

'Ralph's certainly won you around,' Fae said to her.

'Much like his owner has won *you* around,' Sasha quipped back.

She'd walked right into that one…

'You do seem very happy beneath the nerves,' Gigi commented, her observation softer than Sasha's. 'You have a lightness about you, a glow.'

Likely the same glow Rick had mentioned. Nothing to do with Bondi, and everything to do with him.

'It's true, the last month has been…' She searched for one word to sum it up and failed. 'I don't know how to describe it. He's like no one else I've ever known. He makes me feel like no one else. He's so thoughtful, and generous, and kind. He makes me laugh. And he can cook, which is a huge bonus when I can't. Don't get me wrong, he also drives me crazy at times and if he offers to pay for— *What?*'

They were sharing a look, their eyes sparkling, their lips pressed together.

'Why are you looking at each other like that?'

'You sound like…' Sasha said to Gigi.

'She does,' Gigi agreed.

'I what?'

They both looked to her.

'You sound like you're falling in love, Fae-Fae,' her sister cooed.

'Give over.'

Though wasn't her sister saying everything she already knew, had already thought, and just cemented it in her mind?

'It's been a month, sis! You can't fall in love in a month!'

Sasha's eyes widened, Gigi's too. 'Did you—She just...' She pointed at the screen, looked at Gigi, looked back at the screen and leaned in. 'Fae-Fae, did you just call me sis?'

'I—' She swallowed. 'Yeah, I guess I did.'

Sasha covered her mouth, definite tears filling her eyes now.

'Oh, jeez, don't cry on me, Sash! I won't do it again.'

Her sister was fanning her face now and Gigi was hugging her while grinning wide. 'Don't worry, she's fine, I think you just made her honeymoon.'

'Sorry, Gigi, I didn't mean to steal your thunder.'

'Steal away, I don't mind for that, not one bit.'

'Oh, Fae-Fae, I love you.'

She gave her sister a shaky smile. 'And I love you too.' And she had an awful feeling that for all she said she didn't love Rick. That she couldn't have fallen in love with him after only a month. She did. And there was nothing she could do about it.

She may not belong in the world she was about to step into. *His* world. She loved him.

The question was, could the two mix? She was about to find out.

At least with her sister's help she was as ready as she ever would be.

'And thank you for the help today, I couldn't have done it without you both.'

'Any time, *sis*. Though you should have more faith in yourself—you would have been fine without us. Wouldn't she, Gigi?'

Gigi nodded. 'And can I just say, if he doesn't fall in love with you too, he needs his head examined.'

Fae's heart flipped over. The idea of Rick falling in love with her…she gave a pitched laugh. 'We'll see.'

'Keep us posted,' Sasha said.

'I will.'

'Now go be the best-looking dog walker Bondi Beach has ever seen…'

Walking two dogs while trying to protect her hair and make-up from the sea spray was quite the challenge. Not enough to keep her mind off the nervous churn doing its best to return now that she didn't have Sasha and Gigi to distract her. But she was getting it done with her head held high…

'Hey, miss. Hey! You dropped this.'

'Huh?'

She turned to find a dark-haired guy racing up to her, his curly hair flopping about, a satchel over his shoulder and Precious's garish pink poo bag dispenser in his outstretched hand.

'Oh, wow, thank you, I didn't notice. I must have caught the clasp.'

'No worries.' He flicked his fringe back as he handed it over. 'Happens.'

He was British. English. Nothing like Rick's hoity-toity English though. More down-to-earth. Friendly too. His grin was wide and open. Though he was definitely eyeing her funny, likely wondering what on earth she was doing made up like she was from the neck up, dressed like she was from the neck down.

'Cool dogs,' he remarked.

She smiled. 'This one is my sister's. Her name's Precious. And this one is my...my...' What was Rick? How would he introduce her tonight? As his girlfriend, his partner, his other half? The idea warmed her as she said the same. 'My other half's. His name is Ralph. Say hello, guys.'

'I always fancied a Great Dane myself.'

They gave him an inquisitive sniff as he gave them an awkward pat in return. Strange. Though she supposed it was good to be wary of dogs if you didn't know them personally.

Then his eyes were back on her, just as curious. Oh, right, the make-up versus the outfit. Of course.

'I'm off out,' she said, clipping the tiny bag dispenser back on its ring. 'Hence the OTT top half.'

'Ah, right, gotcha. Going anywhere nice?'

'A gala.'

'Sounds fancy.'

She laughed. 'My sentiments exactly.'

She nipped her lip, thinking how nice it was to talk to someone so obviously on her level and how different she would feel in approximately two hours.

'You don't look too excited about it, if you don't mind me saying. Is it not really your bag?'

'My bag?'

'You know, your scene? You don't seem that into it.'

Her laugh was tighter this time. 'You could say that.'

'Looks like I'm heading your way if you fancy offloading a little. I can promise you a good ear and maybe a few laughs for distraction…?'

Now that did sound good. And perhaps the distraction of some company, practice talking to a friendly stranger, might help prepare her for the evening ahead. And he did seem nice. It would be like old times back in the bar. And perfectly safe walking along the seafront with many others around too.

'Sure, why not? I'm Fae, by the way.'

'It's a pleasure to meet you, Fae. My name's Simon…'

CHAPTER THIRTEEN

RICK ROLLED HIS head on his shoulders. It had been a long day and he was feeling it. But the night was yet young. He needed a shower and to get ready, but he wanted to see Fae first.

He'd called round to Sasha's, but she wasn't there. And Ralph wasn't back at his. He assumed she was still out on their afternoon walk so he was waiting on the front terrace, keeping lookout.

He was worried. He hated how they'd left things the night before. He wanted to clear the air, make sure—

Fae!

She appeared in the distance, Precious and Ralph trotting dutifully just ahead. But she wasn't alone. She was deep in conversation with a guy. A guy who made her laugh suddenly. Rick shifted on his feet, shook off the strange feeling trying to work its way in.

You can't be jealous of another guy for making her laugh.

No. But then the closer they got, the more the

unease grew. There was something about him. Something familiar. Something...

What in the hell!

He was down the steps and out of the gate in a flash, upon them before he could draw a full breath.

'Fae!'

'Rick, you're home!' Her smile froze on her lips as her eyes met his. 'Everything okay?'

No, nothing was okay.

And when he didn't reply she turned to her companion. 'This is—'

'I know who this is.'

'You do?'

She looked from him to Simon and back again, a frown forming as the other guy took a step back. 'Lord Pennington, it's good to see you looking so well. Bondi Beach certainly suits you.'

'It certainly doesn't suit you.' Rick ignored the hand Simon proffered and took Fae by the elbow. 'Now if you don't mind, we have somewhere we need to be.'

Not that he cared if the guy minded; he was already marching Fae and the dogs back to the house.

'Rick, you're hurting me.'

He slackened his grip with a grimace, wishing for the life of him that he could be calmer, more in control, but his brain was racing. So many scenarios. So many stories.

What could she have told Simon?

The second they were inside Sasha's domain, she rounded on him. 'What the hell was that about?'

He raked an unsteady hand through his hair. Tried to remind himself that this was Fae, not some money-hungry acquaintance or an untrustworthy peer from his past—*Fae!*

'He's a reporter from the British press. He works for the *Daily Tattle*.'

She froze and he imagined that beneath the carefully applied make-up she paled. Though the make-up was a perfect mask. Quite exquisite too. The smoky eyeshadow drawing out the golden hue to her eyes…which now flared back at him. Shocked. Hurt.

She wet her lips, their glossy pink finish unaffected by the move.

'A reporter?' she whispered, clutching at her stomach.

'A reporter who you seemed pretty quick to bond with. What was it? His looks or his voice that worked in his favour?'

'Rick!'

Inside, his head was screaming at him to take it back, but his heart…his heart hurt.

She was shaking her head, her eyes wide and wounded. 'I had no idea, I swear it.'

'He was drilling you for a story, Fae.'

'But I… But he was nice. He…he…' She looked

to the dogs, who were drinking at their bowls. 'He was asking about the dogs and the gala and...'

'And?'

'Us.'

'Us?'

'You.'

His gut rolled. 'What did you tell him?'

'I... I don't know. I told him that you hadn't been here long. That you were from the UK. That we'd met only recently.'

'What else?'

She started to tremble, the stress emanating off her in waves. 'I don't know. Stuff. Nothing big. He was nice and he was making me feel better about going tonight. Making me feel confident about how I looked and...and telling me that I shouldn't be nervous.'

'But what about my family and my father, the title...?'

'I don't think I mentioned any of that.' And then her frown deepened. '*Why* would I mention any of that?'

He stepped closer. 'You don't think, or you know?'

'I know I didn't.'

'Are you *sure*? Reporters are skilled at getting the information they want out of people unawares.'

She reacted as though slapped, her head flicking back. '*Yes*, he made me feel at ease. *Yes*, I enjoyed his company. I didn't suddenly become an untrustworthy gossip, Rick.'

'I got enough out of you once you got over your first impression, and you had no such qualms with him.'

'The stuff I told you was about *me*, and nobody else. It was mine to share.'

She couldn't have been any clearer or more reassuring. It was him that was jumping to conclusions. Seeing red having seen Simon. So why were his shoulders still around his ears?

'Oh, my God!'

Her exclamation drew him up short. 'What?'

'You don't trust me, do you?'

He stared at her, his little pixie with her fists on her hips, her wild pink hair tamed by a single silver clasp to one side... Breathtakingly beautiful and spitting fire.

'Rick, answer me!'

'I *want* to trust you, Fae. I do.'

'But you don't.'

'I trusted before...'

'And you were burnt. Yes, we've done that discussion to death.'

'And I'm trying...'

'You need to try a hell of a lot harder because this...this doesn't work if that trust is all one-sided.'

And then she spun away. 'Come, Precious, it's bedtime.'

'But Fae, the gala…?'

'I'll see you outside at six.'

How could she have been so foolish?

Actually, scratch that, Fae knew well enough. Rick was right. Her prejudice had risen up to bite her on the arse. She'd *assumed* Simon was a good 'un, based on his voice, his looks, his presumed similarity to her…so different to her present company.

She glanced across at Rick in the back of the swanky car that had been hired to take them to the opera house. His face was angled away, his attention on his phone as it had been for the entire journey. He *looked* busy, but was he?

Or was he just avoiding her?

She was the woman who had betrayed him by getting all cosy with the reporter. She gritted her teeth and looked to the window. When she thought back over her conversation with Simon now, the warning signs had been there. How he'd kept bringing the conversation back to her. Much like Rick had done, but in Simon's case, she hadn't questioned it; she'd gone along with it.

Thankfully, she hadn't given anything incriminating away. Well, nothing other than her relationship to Rick. And if she was honest with herself, she wasn't so sure she'd got that right anymore.

If he didn't trust her, what did they have really?

It was that doubt that stopped her from speaking up in the privacy of the backseat.

And it was that doubt that made her hesitate now as the car pulled up at their destination and the door was opened for her.

Should she just stay where she was and tell him to go without her? *Before* they stepped out in public and the whole world questioned it.

She turned to suggest as much but he'd already gone. Seat empty. His masculine scent on the air. She breathed it in and turned...

You can do this.

She stepped out, her eyes lifting to take in the Sydney Opera House, which gleamed in all its glory, the sail-shaped roofs flaunting the evening sun. She wished she could be a fraction as impressive because though she wore Rick's wealth like a cloak, his money couldn't buy what her heart truly desired and without it, she felt bare. Vulnerable. And terrified of joining all the others who were making their way inside, every one of them as elegant and sophisticated as him. Every one of them belonged here.

Rick arrived at her side, his hand gentle on her arm, and her gaze leapt to his, desperately tried to read his.

The storm had lifted, but in its place was a clear kind of torment. She wasn't sure which irked her more. And then he leaned in close, and her heart stopped.

'I'm sorry, Fae.'

'*You* are?'

He nodded.

'It's…it's okay.' She licked her lips, unnerved but grasping at the unexpected olive branch. 'I should have been more aware.'

'No.' His jaw pulsed. 'I should have warned you that he might be lurking around.'

'You *knew*?'

'Geoffrey mentioned that he might come out here looking for a scoop. I didn't think any more on it until I saw him with you and I… I jumped to conclusions. I'm sorry.'

She huffed, her smile as weak as her knees. 'You're talking to the right person when it comes to jumping to conclusions. I've learned my lesson there.'

His mouth twitched, his tormented gaze keeping her in its grip. Did he not believe her?

'I've called in a few favours. Whatever story he thinks he has, he'll struggle to find a home for it. You should warn your friends and family to be on their guard. I'm afraid your association to me makes you of interest to them now.'

She hadn't even thought…hadn't even considered…

'Is that what you were doing just now?'

'Yes. I couldn't bear it if you got hurt in the crossfire.'

Her heart swelled with his concern. 'I'll warn them.'

'Good.'

And for the first time since they had come together again since their fight, she took a full breath and allowed herself to drink him in. The carefully groomed stubble and the swept back hair with its misbehaving strands that fell forward, framing his impassioned gaze. The dark suit that was cut to enhance his frame. The crisp white shirt, smooth against his front. And the tie that made her want to wrap her hand around it and tug him in so that she might kiss his lips. A real kiss-and-make-up session—not that she dared in such company.

He was so deeply, darkly sexy and she knew every eye, male or female, would be drawn to him tonight, whether he was commanding the room or not.

And he was her date. *Hers!*

She glanced around at the cameras that lined the entrance and the people milling about. The people who *did* belong... She tried to tell herself that she did too.

Channel Sasha!

Don't you dare, Fae-Fae, she imagined her sister saying. *You be you!*

Then came Gigi. *'If he doesn't fall in love with you, too, he needs his head examined.'*

If only.

'Fae…'

Her gaze snapped back to his. He sounded raw, hoarse…his blue eyes blazing as they dipped over her. And she realized this was the first time he'd looked at her properly too. No phone. No distractions.

'My God…'

He said no more for several seconds, *did* nothing more, until she could no longer stand it.

'Rick?'

He blinked, blinked again, his eyes returning to her face. 'You are… There are no words.'

She tilted her head, lifted the skirt out. 'Please give me *something* so that I at least know I'm on the right track.'

'If I wasn't hosting tonight, I'd be taking that track back to our car so we can go home and I can show you just how right it is. You look…ethereal. And every man and woman here tonight will struggle to take their eyes off you.'

She gave a choked laugh. 'I was thinking the same about you.'

He pulled her to him. 'They won't see me for you.'

And then he lowered his mouth to hers. 'Rick…' She pressed him back. 'There are people.'

'And?'

He gave a wolfish grin and kissed her deeply. She was vaguely aware of camera flashes going off, the murmurs of the people, and her cheeks burned, but that burn had nothing on the electrifying effect of his lips against hers.

She may not have his trust yet, but they had this. She could cling to this…take strength from this…couldn't she?

CHAPTER FOURTEEN

'WELL, I'LL BE! I wasn't expecting to see this kind of display on my arrival.'

Rick broke away from Fae to find Geoffrey, grinning ear to ear at their side, an earpiece in, phone in hand. All set to stay on top of the event as well as Rick's life simultaneously.

Though the most important life event was clearly taking place in front of him judging by his PA's face.

'Fae, I'd like you to meet Geoffrey. Geoffrey, this is Fae Thompson, my date.'

Fae's eyes sparkled up at Rick before she turned to greet him. 'It's lovely to meet you at last. I've heard so much about you.'

'And I wish I could say the same about you, but this one keeps his cards close to his chest.'

'Geoffrey.'

The warning in Rick's tone was unmistakeable but his PA waved a nonchalant hand. 'Yes. Yes. Behave. I know. Says the man who was just seen by all and sundry sharing some extreme PDA.'

Fae stifled a giggle and even Rick smiled. 'It's my party. I can kiss who I want to.'

Geoffrey's eyes bulged. 'Oh. My. God. You really did find a life in Bondi. Wait until Kate hears this.'

'And I say again, whose PA are you?'

He wagged a finger. 'Ah-ah, you don't scare me anymore, sir.' He sent a wink Fae's way. 'Okay, maybe he does a little, he does pay the bills after all. Now shall we get inside before your guests drink *all* the champagne...?'

Rick shook his head as Fae chuckled. Never mind Bondi going to his head, Australia had clearly done something to Geoffrey's.

'I like him. A lot,' Fae murmured as they followed Geoffrey inside.

'Something tells me he already likes you a lot too.'

Once inside, they mixed and mingled with the masses in the lead-up to his welcome speech. The Hamiltons were noticeably absent but then he wasn't surprised; Zara liked to be fashionably late and make an entrance of her entrance.

Which was all he needed...

'Are you ready for your speech, sir?' Geoffrey came up to them, a fresh glass of champagne in each hand, which he offered out. 'Most of the guests are here.'

Rick scanned the room and noticed Fae was doing the same. She'd only met half the room.

Was she trying to work out which one was Zara? Should he save her the trouble and tell her she wasn't—

Ah, never mind, there was a flurry of activity at the door, the Hamiltons had just arrived and Zara was straight out in front.

'And here I was hoping she might have been taken sick last minute,' Geoffrey murmured under his breath as they watched the woman take a glass of champagne from an approaching waiter.

'Geoffrey…'

'I know, behave.'

'Is that…?'

'Zara Hamilton, indeed,' Geoffrey said to Fae, 'aka the devil reincarnate.'

Fae gazed across the room at the statuesque blonde dressed in scarlet red. And she wasn't the only one. Every eye in the room seemed to swivel her way as Fae's heart sank into her stomach.

She was everything Fae wasn't.

Older. Richer. Classier. So at ease with the attention. So at one with the elegance of the room…

And he'd been engaged to this woman? Would have married this woman? Did Fae honestly think he would ever do the same with her?

'Fae?'

'Huh?'

'I asked if you'd be okay while I do my speech.'

Get a grip, Fae. He's with you, not her. He

chose you. Not her. He could have asked her. He asked you.

'Of course.' She sipped at her drink, her eyes drifting back towards Zara and struggling to see her through all the men who had now flocked to her side. If she was lucky, Australia's eligible bachelors would keep the woman suitably distracted and busy the entire night!

'I'll be back as soon as I can.'

He swept a chaste kiss against her cheek and she watched him go. Focused on him and his speech. Lost herself in a side to Rick she hadn't yet seen. He was a charming host, captivating the masses with such effortless ease. But then it made sense, he'd been born into this.

As for his obvious passion, the charity wasn't just close to his heart; it *was* his heart? The hereditary disease brought tears to her eyes now and she dabbed at the corner of her eyes, praying no one else would see.

'He's good, isn't he?' Geoffrey said as he appeared at her side, discreetly handing her a handkerchief.

She nodded.

'As are you. I never thought I'd see the day he'd smile or joke or laugh like he has since you came into his life. You've cast some kind of spell over him, Miss Thompson.'

She choked on her bubbles and the unshed tears.

'You're giving me too much credit.'

'And you're not giving yourself enough.'

Geoffrey gave her a warm smile.

'Right, that's the welcome over with,' Rick said, returning to their side.

'Not quite. You still have a few latecomers to meet, including you know who…'

Rick's smile twisted. 'I suppose I must.'

'It will be noticed if you don't.'

Rick turned to her. 'But only if you're okay with it.'

She nodded, hooking her arm in his. 'Of course.'

He covered her hand upon his arm and she lifted her chin as they followed Geoffrey through the crowd.

You've got this, she told herself. *You look the part so* feel *the part.*

Though every step, she felt the spike of her heel. Unsteady. Teetering. The eyes were turning. From Zara, to them, to Fae.

She could feel their gaze sweeping over her, assessing her. Did they know who Zara was to Rick? Were they comparing them both? Finding Fae lacking?

Her knees trembled as the slit in the gown permitted her every step and she fought the urge to draw it together, to prevent them from seeing. She tried to take a breath, but the bodice that had felt made-to-fit only hours ago now squeezed at her ribs. Her skin felt hot and clammy.

'You look stunning.'

His words brushed like a caress against her ear, triggering a tiny tremor through her middle and a smile from the depths of her despair.

'You scrub up well yourself.'

He chuckled softly and then Zara's eyes found his as she gifted him a smile for him alone, shattering the moment so completely. Her eyes drifted to Fae on his arm and something flickered across her face—pain, distaste, jealousy… Whatever the cause, her smile never wavered but her eyes said it all.

She turned to her neighbour, said something before weaving through the crowd towards them.

Geoffrey stepped forward to run the introductions, but she swatted him aside. 'Cedric, darling, it's so good to see you…' Blood-red nails clawed his upper arms as she leaned in to peck his cheek, her perfume unnecessarily cloying—or was that just the effect of her presence? Provoking Fae's inferiority complex and a jealousy she didn't want to acknowledge or feel?

'And who is this…sweet little thing?'

Sweet little thing… It made her think of Rick and his pixie penchant. But he wasn't belittling her. *She* was. Zara. And she hated the woman for tainting it now. Hated it even as she pinned a smile to her face.

'This is Fae. Fae, this is Zara. Daughter of Sir Hamilton, our prestigious benefactor.'

Was he trying to make her feel better by qualifying Zara's presence here by association with her father?

Zara gave a soft chuckle. 'My, my, Cedric, I'm a little more than that, wouldn't you say…'

Rick stiffened and Fae touched a hand to his arm, a silent communication not to worry. She had this. She hoped.

'I trust you are having a pleasant evening, Lady Zara.' She wanted to vom at the words coming out of her mouth, but she was determined to play nice and play the role expected of her.

Zara's eyes narrowed to slits and then she cackled. *Truly* cackled.

What had she said? Done even?

Her inferiority complex rose to greet the laughter head on, and Rick might as well have been made of stone for all he was moving now.

'I'm not a *lady*, darling. My father is Sir Hamilton, my mother is called Lady Hamilton but alas, I am simply Zara. Oh, my, Cedric, you must teach her some etiquette for when you return to England. You know how cruel some people can be.'

Fae's cheeks burned deeper with every word, her gut shrivelling to the size of a walnut. If only the ground could open up and take her…

'Perhaps it's you—' Geoffrey started and Rick stepped in.

'Perhaps it is you who needs to learn some etiquette,' he said through gritted teeth. 'And do close your mouth, Zara, you wouldn't want to ruin your appetite with a predinner fly. Now if you will excuse us, we have other people to greet.'

They moved on swiftly, Geoffrey positively vibrating with glee. 'Just when I thought I couldn't love you more, sir.'

'Yes, well, maybe next year we'll reconsider having a blacklist.'

'Excellent idea.'

'I wish I'd thought to come out with that,' Fae murmured to Rick.

'I'm just sorry you had to endure it. Please forget everything she said.'

'Consider it forgotten.' The laughter though… she could still hear it ringing in her ears, just like when she was fourteen, only so much worse.

'Now allow me to introduce you to our next guests…' Geoffrey said pausing beside another group of people who stopped conversing at their arrival and started to turn. 'This is esteemed surgeon, Mr Fraser Manders. His wife, Martina. And daughters Eloise, Florence and Grace.'

With open horror, Fae stared at her father, his wife and his daughters. The other family. Her worst nightmare. And the glass in her hand fell and shattered with her heart…

Rick watched her crumple. Physically she was still standing but everything about her had shrunk. Her light, her confidence, her energy.

'Fae…?' He reached out but she shook him off as a waiter rushed up with a dustpan and brush.

'I'm so sorry,' she blurted, her eyes failing to make contact with anyone as she apologized and ran, pushing her way free of the group and then the room.

'Fae!'

She didn't stop.

'Fae!'

She kept on going, falling over her own feet, shrugging off his hand when he tried to make her pause.

'Fae!'

It wasn't until she was outside that she rounded on him, her eyes wild, chest heaving. 'How *could* you?'

'How could I what? I don't…'

And then the pieces started to fall into place, his gut lurching with them… The surgeon. The man and his family.

No, please, God, no.

'He's my father,' she whispered through quivering lips, tears filling up her eyes.

'Fae…' It was an anguished groan as he threw his hands into his hair, grasping handfuls when all he wanted was to take hold of her. 'I didn't know. I swear it! You *have* to believe me. If I had known, I *never* would have invited him.'

'Really?' A choked scoff. 'No blacklist, remember? Money's money, and he has plenty of it.'

'I wouldn't have taken *his* and put you through this. I *swear* it! You have to believe me!'

'You take Sir Hamilton's!'

'That's different. That's my past, my pain to deal with.'

'Your pain?'

'You know what I mean.'

'Do I? I don't know what to think anymore.'

'I'm so sorry, Fae.'

'Are you? You're the one who brought me here. You're the one who gave me all the money for my heart's desire and dressed me up like one of you. Made me like *her*...'

She choked on the last, openly crying now, tears streaming down her face. Mascara running. It killed him to see her in so much pain. Pain that he had caused.

'You once told me not to change for anyone or anything and this isn't me, and yet you gave me your money and told me to change.'

'I didn't. I told you to get yourself something nice for an event. I couldn't care what you wore, so long as you were happy. Hell, you could have come in your shorts and T and I would have been just as proud to show you off.'

She choked on a laugh. 'Yeah, right.'

'I'm not kidding, Fae. We would have had some funny looks, but I'd have walked in there, head held high because yours was...'

She shook her head, eyes wide and disbelieving. 'I can't do this, Rick.'

He stepped forward, softened his voice, held his hand out hoping that she'd meet him halfway. 'I know. I don't expect you to go back in there now. I wish I could go home with you. The last thing I want to do is leave you after the shock you've had but—'

'No, you don't understand. I can't do *this*! Me and you.'

His throat closed over. She couldn't be serious. 'Fae, it's been a hell of a night. Once you've had time—'

'Time isn't going to change the fact that we don't belong together.'

'You can't mean that.'

'But I do!'

'Please Fae, don't do this.'

'Don't do what? Don't end this relationship before you have a chance to end it further down the line when you realize what my father did, that I'm not good enough. Worthy enough to choose. Did you *see* them? His…his *daughters*! Did you see how perfect and beautiful they were? Did you see how they looked at me? And did you see his face? The recognition and then, the *disgust*.'

'It looked more like fear to me.'

'Whatever it was, it wasn't love.'

'Fae, please.' He took another step and she backed up, stumbling in her heels.

'Don't, Rick.' Her eyes were frenzied, desperate. He knew her head wasn't fully in the present. That right now, he wasn't sure who she was seeing, who she was fighting, him or her father, but he wanted to wrap her in his arms. Whisper sweet nothings until she calmed. Anything but this…

'Let me be there for you.'

'No. I need to go, and you have a gala to get back to. I won't ruin your night any more than I already have. Goodbye, Rick.'

And then she swept away, her farewell as final as one could be, and he watched her go. Unsure of how long he stood there for but eventually he returned to the gala in a daze.

Most people gave him the decency of space as a sympathetic Geoffrey sidled up to him, but her father had other ideas. He made a beeline straight for him as he left his baffled wife and daughters behind.

Bring it on, thought Rick. He had plenty to say to the man. Like how he could think for a second that his money could replace the love his daughter had so desperately craved and deserved all her life…?

And that's when it hit him, his epic blunder. He'd been no better than her own father all along. Showering her with his wealth when he should have been showering her in his affection, his… *love*.

He hadn't found a life worth living because of

Bondi; he'd found it because of her. Fae. His sweet little… His fists clenched as he thought of the words Zara had twisted but he was determined to reclaim them. Because Fae was his sweet little pixie goddess and she was his one true love.

And he hadn't told her.

But he would.

Just as soon as he could.

CHAPTER FIFTEEN

'HEY, DARL, COME HERE.'

Poor Precious seemed to be suffering with empathy for Fae the next morning. Not only had she sicked up her breakfast, what little she had eaten, but she was also totally uninterested in leaving the house.

After a quick Google, Fae had decided it was likely nothing to worry about, but she'd keep a close eye on her all the same. And so they had curled up on the sofa and watched the sunrise from there, Fae stroking at her fur and finding some comfort in the company. Though her mind was restless, replaying the night's events over and over.

She'd have to message Sasha and Gigi at some point. The pair would start to hound her soon for an update—that's if the gossip tabloids didn't get there first! It was one thing for Rick to try to stop Simon circulating anything, but an entire room of partygoers sharing the scene she had made…

She swallowed back the nausea, but nothing could beat back the desperate ache within her chest. She'd heard his car return in the early hours and her ears had strained for footsteps on the path, her heart pleading for him to come her way.

He hadn't. He'd done as she had asked. Let her end it.

But she'd been so jacked up on the pain of her past.

No, the pain of her past *and* her present. Both colliding in such a way that she hadn't been able to think clearly, let alone process her feelings enough to tell him what truly mattered.

That she loved him. That against the backdrop of all that glamour, the only reason it hurt so much was because she feared she couldn't be enough for him. And the idea that she would love him and that he would in turn reject that love…she hadn't been able to bear it.

Precious whimpered in her lap. 'I know, honey, I was a wuss.'

The poodle made the same sound, longer this time, lifting her head further, her tail beating against the sofa.

'What is it?'

Fae looked to the sliding doors and the steps that led down to the front gate as Precious dropped to the floor and trotted up to the glass. Rick? Was it possible?

She stood. Started to walk. Precious barked. She checked her watch. It wasn't yet seven in the morning…would he really call now?

She stared out. Nothing. No buzz of the intercom. No movement. Yet the poodle's tail still wagged.

'They've probably gone for their walk, darl.'

She stroked her head, started to turn away when Precious barked and ran through the gap she'd left open in the door...

One of you has the right idea, came her inner conscience. *Get after him and tell him the truth.*

She thought of how she'd felt when those footsteps hadn't come her way and knew she couldn't wait on him. This was on her.

Heart in throat, she grabbed Precious's lead and raced out, uncaring that she was shoeless and still in her threadbare PJs. The only sight she cared about was him.

Latching Precious onto the lead, she threw open the gate and launched forward, straight into a solid wall of muscle. Strong hands gripped her arms before she could rebound onto her butt.

'Fae!'

'Rick!'

She blinked up at him. Crumpled and creased in the suit from the gala, tie stripped, shirt unbuttoned at the collar, hair askew, eyes shadowed. 'You look like hell!'

And yet, he still looked better than any other man alive.

His mouth quirked to one side. 'I've yet to see a bed...'

'But… I heard you come home in the night.'

'I sent Geoffrey home for Ralph. I knew I couldn't come home and not come straight here. I was right. Case in point.'

He lifted his hands out and her body instantly missed the warmth of his touch as she wrapped her arms around her middle. 'But where did you stay?'

His eyes flared. 'Not with *her* if that's what you're worrying about.'

'God, no. I just meant…'

'I had Geoffrey's hotel room, but I didn't use it. I walked until the sun started to rise and then I got a cab. And now I'm here because I have to tell you what I should have told you last night.'

She swallowed. 'And what's that?'

He lifted his hand to her face, stroked his thumb along her cheek, his blue eyes searing in the golden hue of the morning sun. 'I love you, Fae. And I'm sorry I didn't just shout it after you last night, but I do.'

Laughter bubbled up within her. Delicious. Joyous. Disbelieving.

He frowned. 'What's so funny?'

'I don't believe it.'

'Well, it's the truth.'

And still she laughed, so light and so happy and…

'Not the reaction I was expecting.' He scratched

the back of his head. 'No, seriously, Fae, I need you to listen to me.'

'I am listening, and that's not what I don't believe, though it is rather surreal.'

'Then what is...?'

She slipped her fingers into his hair. 'It's that you took the words right out of my mouth. That *I* should have told you the exact same thing last night. That I realized my mistake the second I got away. That of all the things I had told you, I hadn't told you the most important thing...that I love *you*.'

'You do? After everything I got wrong? Throwing money at you, thinking it was the answer to everything, your nerves about the gala, meeting Zara... I hadn't stopped to think that what you were truly lacking was me. After everything you'd told me of your father, of growing up too... I couldn't believe I'd be so thoughtless, so heartless.'

'You're not heartless, Rick, you're never heartless.'

'No? I was plenty heartless when it came to telling you how I felt. Because I don't think I realized myself how deep my feelings ran until I was forced to watch you walk away from me. Because I love you, from the bottom of my heart, I love you.'

His words seeped beneath her skin, permeating her heart and warming her through.

'I love you, too. And I'm sorry I ran from you and that I ruined your gala.'

He went to interject, but she touched a finger to his lips. 'It's my turn to explain. I just couldn't bear it, being in the same room as him, as you. Realizing I was in the same impossible situation, craving love from a man who couldn't return it.' He hesitated beneath her finger, his lashes flickering over eyes that blazed with his love. 'Only this time it was worse, because this time I not only loved that man, he was worthy of it too. Because I do love you, Rick, and you really are worthy of it.'

She slipped her finger away and kissed him softly.

'I'm so sorry you had to face him,' he murmured fervently against her lips, his arms slipping around her waist. 'If I could go back and change it…'

'You weren't to know.'

'Well, I do know now, and he knows my feelings very well. He'll be making his donations from a distance in the future.'

'What did you say to him?'

'Nothing that wasn't warranted and nothing that would cause you or your mother any harm, I promise.'

'And his family?'

'Still blissfully unaware. That's his own bed to deal with.'

She nodded. 'So he'll continue donating if you…'

'No, Fae, I would never resort to blackmail. If

he wants to assume such a thing then that's down to him.'

She nodded, her stomach swimming with it all.

'But I really don't want to talk of him anymore, do you?'

'Absolutely not.'

'I'd suggest we get Ralph from Geoffrey and take them for a walk, but I could really use a shower...'

'I'm not sure a walk is on the cards. Precious is behaving a little off this morning. Though she perked up a little with your arrival...'

He looked at the fluffy white pooch who in the time they'd been talking had dropped back to lie down.

'Maybe she's missing Ralph. Tell you what, come back to mine, we'll shower there...'

'*We'll* shower?'

'Do you think I'm letting you out of my sight when I've only just got you back?'

'What about Geoffrey?'

'He'll be too relieved to see you again to pass comment.'

She laughed. 'How about we go get Ralph and then we'll shower here instead?'

'Deal.'

EPILOGUE

One month later

'DARLING, I KNOW you're smitten, but can I steal you for a second…?'

Fae could barely tear her eyes away as she sat cross-legged on the floor. She *was* smitten. Head over heels, one hundred per cent in love with seven tiny fur balls.

The last few weeks had been a blur. With Sasha's return from her honeymoon being delayed due to a freak storm in the Caribbean, there hadn't been a 'right' time to explain about Precious's condition, which had become apparent after the gala. A bit of extra googling and they'd booked her straight in with Rick's vet for confirmation.

No expense spared for Sasha's darling.

And though Fae felt immensely guilty that she hadn't told Sasha, ever more so that it had all happened on her watch, the idea of delivering the news over the phone or video call felt wrong, especially when there was nothing her sister could do to get home any faster.

She just had to hope that she took it well. Though one look at Precious nursing her babies, how could Sasha not melt on the spot?

'I can lend you an ear,' she compromised as Rick wrapped an arm around her middle and eased her to her feet.

'A man can get jealous, you know.'

She laughed as she turned into him. 'What about a dog? Look at poor Ralph—he doesn't know where to put himself.'

'I know how he feels.'

She looped her hands around his neck and kissed his pout away. 'You're not really jealous.'

'Of course not, but I do need to talk to you about something before your sister arrives. Because I have a feeling once she gets here we won't have much opportunity for talk and this is important.'

His sudden severity had her stiffening, her heart thudding in her chest. 'What's wrong?'

'Come with me.' He took her by the hand and led her into the front room.

'You're worrying me. Is it the doctor? Has something changed...?'

'No, nothing like that, not really...' He paused in the middle of the room and turned to her.

'Not really?' That was hardly reassuring. She covered her throat with her palm.

'Look I know when we got together, that kids were not on your radar and that suited me just fine. But I've watched you this past week. I've seen you with those pups, and you're so soft, Fae. So soft and loving and I don't know, the idea that you and I…' He raked a hand through his hair. 'Because of the risks.'

She stepped up to him, placed her hand over his heart as she realized where he was heading with this. 'You can't choose the heart you fall in love with, Rick, and I choose yours. I fell in love with yours.'

'But what of the future, of our children if we were to reconsider…'

A smile played about her lips. She had been thinking along the same lines. The future filling up with possibility the day she had let their love colour it pretty. 'About that… I've been meaning to talk to you too.'

'You've changed your mind?'

She nodded. 'More than just changed it. I want lots, Rick. Lots and lots. I want to love as many as I can in this one lifetime.'

His brows disappeared into his hair line as he choked out, 'Okay, now you're scaring me. I know the risk doesn't increase with each child but…'

She gave a soft laugh. 'Not quite what I was meaning… How would you feel about fostering? We have the most glorious location for any home.

We have the stability. You have the means and I have the time…'

'But what about all your talk of going back to school, of counselling, or maybe even opening a bar of your own?'

'They were all ideas that centred around my past. This is about the future and what I truly want to fill it with. And that's love. Our love. And I want to give a home to kids who for whatever reason don't have that in their lives. I want to make them feel wanted and loved again. I know it'll be hard and come with challenges of its own and there'll be lessons to be learned along the way. But it's something I'd like to explore…if it's something you would like to explore too.'

His blue eyes were awash with something. She just wasn't sure what. Shock, maybe?

'Please say something.'

'I never thought I could love you more.'

She huffed out a relieved breath. 'Does that mean you'll think about it?'

'I'll do more than think about it. I'll make some calls first thing tomorrow, while you're out with your sister and Gigi.'

'Really?'

'Really.'

She reached up on tip toes, kissed him with all the gratitude and love she felt inside. Contemplated whether now was the time to ask if they could keep a puppy or two as well, but…baby steps.

'And while we're on the future,' he broke away to say, 'there's just one more thing I need to ask and then you can go back to your four-legged babies…'

'Anything!'

'In that case, Fae, my spirited pixie…'

She gasped as he dropped to one knee, the sun's rays lighting up his eyes as out of the back pocket of his jeans he lifted up a ring box.

'There will be those who say it's too soon and pass judgement on us before we can prove our worth. But I don't care, because when you know, you know, and the only judgement I care about is yours.' Then he grinned. 'Besides, they'll soon come around to what beats beneath the surface— you sure did.'

She gave a choked laugh. 'I can't believe you're managing to make a proposal about me and my prejudice!'

He shrugged. 'Isn't that what they're supposed to be about? The "you" bit, that is. So what do you say, will you do me the honour of becoming my wife?'

She grinned wide. 'Yes, Rick! Yes!' She swooped down to hug him to her, tears streaming down her cheeks. 'Of course, I'll be your wife!'

'Fae-Fae, we're home! Oh, my God!' There was a squeal, followed by another, and Fae and Rick leapt apart, eyes wide on the door to the kitchen. *'Fae!'*

Fae looked at Rick. 'Uh-oh, do you think she's found them?'

Rick looked at Fae. 'What do you think?'

They scrambled to their feet and raced into the kitchen to find Gigi and Sasha standing over Mum, proud Dad and the babies…

'Hey sis!' Fae gave a sheepish wave. 'Meet the newest additions to the family, your Great Danoodles! You always said you wanted a big family, right?'

One big *happy* family…or it would be, once her sister came down off the ceiling.

* * * * *

If you enjoyed this story,
check out these other great reads
from Rachael Stewart

Fake Fling with the Billionaire
Unexpected Family for the Rebel Tycoon
Reluctant Bride's Baby Bombshell
My Unexpected Christmas Wedding

All available now!